Endorsements

Avonvale is a historical romance full of hope. Andrea has painted a portrait of faith and love in the act of conquering the barriers life presents.

—*Jan Parker, free-lance journalist, novelist*

A. J. Clements is so good at creating imagery with layered descriptions. All of her characters are so endearing. I just loved Avonvale and truly didn't want it to end.

—*Andrea Owens, singer/songwriter/actress/playwright*

Andrea Clements has come out with a bang-up first novel. Twists, turns, love and adventure, all the ingredients of historical fiction, spring from the pages. Her novel spans the countries of Ireland and America. Avonvale is a story of a young couple, Tom and Mary, who must come to grips with the trials and rewards of their relationship as well as the demands of a new country. Horse lovers, history lovers and romantics will find Andrea's novel charming.

—*Trish Sheppard, Artist/poet/writer*

Andrea's first novel is an easy read with a good pace and is full of show, don't tell. She did a superb job of researching the history, places and time span throughout three generations. Her use of dialogue is excellent and aids to moving the story along well. I look forward to reading more from this author.

—*Lawrence Lilienthal, Sr., Author/editor*

AVONVALE

an Irish story

For Marilyn —
Hope you enjoy my story.
Andrea

A.J. Clements

A. J. CLEMENTS

Avonvale

©2020, A. J. Clements

ANTRIM PRESS

ISBN: 978-1-09833-598-4
ISBN eBook: 978-1-09833-599-1

This book is dedicated to my children, Heather and Ben,
With Love.

Acknowledgments

Most importantly, I thank God. Writing my book has definitely been a joint effort.

I want to thank my sister, Gail, for her love, encouragement and for always believing in me.

Thank you to my beta readers and critique group: Andrea Owens, Jan Parker, Trish Sheppard and Larry Lilienthal. Your feedback has been invaluable during my journey through Avonvale.

Thank you to Michael Lees and Heather MacIntyre for working with me to create my book cover design.

Thank you to Lisa Bisbee for helping me on this journey of book publishing. To you, my friend, thank you for inspiring me to feel joy when I felt doubt.

I will always be grateful to Bernie Hale, my first editor, my friend, who I love and laughed with while he helped me delete all the "fluff" early on.

Thank you to my family and friends who continued to cheer me on and support my dream for Avonvale.

To Matthew O'Brien, my teammate, thank you for your unconditional love every day and your constant support throughout my creation of Avonvale.

Thank you for always telling me, "*It's a beautiful thing*".

And now these three remain: faith, hope and love. But the greatest of these is love. (1 Corinthians 13:13)

AVONVALE

PART ONE

"Courage, dear heart."
~ C. S. LEWIS

Chapter 1

Irish Heartbeat

Where there was joy is emptiness, echoes of a love left behind.

Mary knew that whispers on the hill and in the valley would now be nonexistent. Her dad tapped his horse with the reins and kissed the air. The old wagon lurched forward. She grabbed the rail beside her, craned her neck, eyes fixed on her mum whose diminutive wave accompanied silent tears.

~

At eighteen, Mary's whole world was changing, and she felt a sense of worry that nothing would ever make her feel safe again. She snapped her head side to side searching for Tom to appear.

Mary's heart took on an unsteady rhythm. "I want to see him — to say goodbye."

Her dad pulled back on the reins, cleared his throat and spoke with a husky, stern voice. "Goodbye isn't what you want, though. Tom's away at a cattle auction. It's best this way, Lass."

Mary thought of that afternoon in the meadow and the delicate, musical song of a skylark as Tom sauntered toward her in the sunlight. The soft glow in his silvery-blue eyes etched their way into her mind.

"I hope I'm not intruding. You look lovely in that yellow dress, Mary. The color suits you, but then I don't know of a color that doesn't."

Mary would always remember her unexpected, searching invitation for him to take her in his arms and make love to her in the meadow. A gentleness in his voice and genuine smile spread across his face turning it from handsome to divine. Even now, the deep sorrow and fear she felt for the upcoming months ahead could not outweigh that afternoon when they lay in each other's arms for the first time. Mary knew she'd love Tom for the rest of her life.

∼

Cricket songs gave way to bird songs as the sun peaked over the horizon. Mary and her dad continued along the worn wagon path with its green ribbon center that distinguished *The Green Road*.

"Dad, I'll be back, won't I?"

He looked ahead and nudged the horse. "When this is over, Lass."

Scattered along the hillside leading to their thatched-roof Tudor farmhouse, showy racemes of white, blue, pink and yellow lupines reached for the sky. She inhaled their sweetness as well as the additional pungent smell of a turf fire rising from the chimney.

The sweeping landscapes of rich greens all faded away as a furrowed dirt road led them through a dense forest. With the warm breeze left behind, Mary was filled with a sense of foreboding. It was as quiet as the sound of falling snow, and as they forged deeper into the woods, the dampness smelled of decay. High above, a canopy of crackling branches touched and barely allowed light to filter through. Dense moss-veiled trails and shadows lurked in the sodden folds.

Sheep and cattle throughout the low sweeping valleys held the only conversations. Half-blown lilting songs of larks and thrushes seemed to melt away with distance. Beyond the trees, Queen Anne's lace now appeared to choke the grassy hills.

Mary's heart picked up a faster rhythm. She thought back to the days when she and Tom were children. She wished they were back there as Sir Gallagher and Lady Arabella, a time when their imaginations carried them soaring through the sky on their mythical winged stallion they called Dreamaker.

~

Mary's breath labored as they approached a stone house with a thatched roof of straw, water reeds and rushes all woven together. One corner of the house seemed to have collapsed inwardly on itself, like a loaf of bread taken out of the oven too soon, she thought. The glass windows were yellow and wavy.

"Come meet the Morrisons, Lass."

Mary's hands slid down from her dad's shoulders, and she hugged him tight. "Please, Dad."

He held her at arm's length. "It's best you settle in. I'll be back to see how you're getting on in about a fortnight when I'm in the area at next auction."

Mary followed his hazel eyes to the distant sky and watched him swallow hard. She knew that wasn't true, and her heart sank further.

"Visits aren't permitted, house rules, sorry," a woman said as she approached them. She curled her arm around Mary's shoulder. "Now, don't you go worrying your wee self. We'll take good care of you. I'm Mrs. Morrison, and you must be Mary."

She nodded to Mary's dad, picked up the suitcase, and they walked toward the house. Mary looked back to see the wagon rumbling along the bumpy road. She let out a breath she didn't know she was holding.

One of the girls stood on the porch. Mary was surprised to see her belly stuck out so far that her skirt appeared much higher in the front.

"Rebecca, please take Mary to your room. I'm sure you and Nancy won't mind sharing with her. Mr. Morrison will bring her suitcase up in short order."

Rebecca gave Mary a callous look and a jab with her elbow. Mary followed.

Chapter 2

For the Love of Mary

Tom was aloft in the barn throwing bales of hay below with a rhythmic, steady pace. The loft was smoky with dust, and combined with a steamy haze from the summer's humidity, it accumulated in layers over his young, strong body. He wiped his forearm across his brow. His thoughts were of the cool rains and Mary.

"Tom, come down here. I need a word."

Tom joined his father leaning against the split-rail fence and gazing across the fields.

"Not too long from now you'll be in charge of all you see here. The land will become a part of you. It will do that to a man. You'll understand this one day. You need to get on with your life, Lad. You and Mary just can't be."

His father's words carried a hollow quality. The very thought of a life without Mary was unimaginable, second cousin or not.

⤳

Before dawn the next day Tom crept through the house. He pulled out the desk chair, sitting half on and half off to avoid adding his weight to the already bowed cane in the seat. It stood caddy-corner beside the archway leading to their family parlor. Tom opened the drop-down desktop which displayed a broken chain on one side. It had been that way as long as he could remember. Tom left a note, picked up his bag and reached for a pear and almond tart. How many times did that sharp slap of the kitchen door follow behind anyone passing through it, he thought. Tom eased the door shut and stood on his dad's white-washed porch.

The rising sun extended its welcoming energy. Tom tipped his head back and felt that this was a positive reinforcement. The screened door swung open.

"What are you doing up, Mikey? Go back to bed," he whispered.

"But I heard mum and dad talking. I know where Mary is."

⤳

Tom walked to the end of The Green Road. Normally, his next step would be to turn right heading for the farmer's market. However, on this particular morning, he turned left toward Belfast along the Antrim Road. The one thing he knew for certain was that Mary could be found with a family on the Crumlin Road just north of Belfast's City Center.

Tom soon heard a strange noise approaching from behind. He moved to the side of the road and turned around to see a shiny, red automobile. An "Aaoogha" sounding noise blared again and again.

"Ahoy," a woman's voice called out. "I'm having trouble stopping this thing."

The vehicle sputtered past him, and when it came to a stop, she waved for him to come ahead. Tom slung the bag over his shoulder and trotted up to the car. So this was the American motorcar he had heard so much about, but what was one doing on the Antrim Road?

"Hope I didn't startle you, young man. Driving this thing isn't as easy as it looks, I assure you. It's like trying to do the Charleston while loading a musket after a big night at the speakeasy." The woman gave him a sassy wink.

She sat tall, a leggy blonde with great style and elegance. Her hair was twisted back into a soft chignon. She wore pearl earrings and white lace, wrist length gloves.

"I'm Edith Sterling and you are?" She leaned across the seat with her palm facing down.

"Tom Clements," he said shaking her hand.

A giggle sneaked past her lips. "Ever see anything like this before? I think red looks quite smart, don't you?"

He scanned the various pedals required to navigate. "It surely does."

"And you are going where?"

"Belfast. I'm meeting with me bride-to-be," he said with a broad smile.

"Well, this is your lucky day. I'm headed for Belfast myself. You can use the ride, and I can use the company. Hop in Tom Clements. You can't keep your bride waiting forever."

Tom tossed his bag in the back and jumped in.

She shifted into first gear, and the car jerked ahead as was the case with the second gear. Edith firmly held the wheel with both hands, rolled her shoulders and narrowed her gaze to a squint.

"How do you like my get up? It's a far cry from those ridiculous motoring clothes. I got rid of the heavy car coat, those unnatural looking dust shields and the hideous driving gloves - so blasé. The fact is, I don't need a signal for being a part of the elite. I just am." She brushed a couple of curls to one side. "May I inquire as to where your home is?"

"Back in Ballymena."

"Oh, I just spent the night at a lovely guest house in your village."

Tom hung onto every word that rolled off her tongue.

"My husband was Sir Edward Sterling, by the way, well-known in Belfast as a shipping tycoon of sorts. He owned boats - lots of them: passenger ships, freighters and escort vessels. And he was as raucous as he was successful. Edward shipped a string of red Model T's to Cork, Belfast and Liverpool from America. He presented me with this fine motorcar and a boatload of money after he left this world for a better place."

Edith focused on the road and sighed. "I had no idea he was sick. He hid it well, and Edward made all the arrangements without me knowing." She blinked rapidly to stave off her tears. "And he was quite properly mourned, I might add."

They rode in silence until Edith angled her head to the right.

"So what did you say her name was?"

"I don't think I did." His eyes sparkled with pride. "It's Mary."

"She has a good Irish name — same as my sister. We'll have a nip, a toast, to our two Marys."

Her eyes fixed on the narrow road as she leaned forward, reached under her seat and removed a silver flask. "Would you mind opening this? And please help yourself while you're at it."

He opened it and handed it back to her. "I think I'm going to pass, thank you."

Extending her pinky, Edith tipped her head back and took a swallow. She grimaced and shook her head. His eyebrows lifted, and his lips curled upward.

"Is she away at school or does she have a job in Belfast?"

"Neither."

"Oh, I know. She was sent away."

"And how'd you know that?" he said in jest.

"It's easy. Look darling, if you've been around as much as I have, you'd know every problem falls into two categories: romances or finances. If a young woman isn't at school, married or working, something's amiss. Ah, she's Catholic, right?"

Tom was quick to answer. "No, she's not a Catholic. We're cousins. Actually, we're second cousins."

Edith slowly nodded her head. "Cousins, huh?" A little smile eased across her mouth. "Are you in love?"

Tom sat back, calm, complacent. "Indeed we are."

"Well, in America, this is not a problem."

He tipped his head to the side and raised an eyebrow. "What does that mean?"

"You ought to go there and find out for yourselves."

Tom noticed that the sheep in a nearby pasture were marked with a splotch of blue paint, except for one who had wandered away from his home. A red splotch identified him to belong with another flock.

A light sweat gathered on his forehead and upper lip. "To be honest, there's a wee bit more to the story," he said.

"She's pregnant?" Edith said.

Tom nodded.

Edith touched her index finger to her chin. "Ahhh, that does complicate things."

"Mary's dad took her to Belfast where she's to have our baby boy, and then he'll be adopted by a Protestant family."

Edith's eyes widened, and a ghost of a smile settled on her lips.

"Now, how would you know it's a boy?"

"I prayed hard, so I know it to be true."

"Very well, then. No need to argue that point. Please continue."

He looked ahead. "There's really nothing more to say."

Edith pulled over at the entrance to a pasture and stopped the car. She placed her hands atop the steering wheel and lay her forehead on top of them. After a few moments, she rolled her head aside to face him.

"What the hell was your name again?"

"Tom Clements."

Edith reached for the flask, opened it and tipped her head back.

"Well, Tom Clements, I think I can be of assistance. So you know, I have friends, James and Edith O'Reilly. They will help you. I'm sure of it, and you can trust them. They live just outside of Belfast on the north side and not out of my way at all. I have known them for a long time, and we'll be at their door in less than an hour."

The wind sighed through the trees as Edith downshifted and entered a quaint valley. Rounding a corner, wild strawberry patches bordered the road along with red stalks of rhubarb which introduced a field of pink Heather in bloom. He was reminded of his mum's strawberry rhubarb pies and of Mary.

Chapter 3
The Mission

They pulled up to a white stonewall, thatched roof bungalow with a red double-hung door. Tom followed Edith up the fieldstone walkway rimmed with yellow Rose of Sharon. He caught a glimpse of someone in the window. Within seconds, the top half of the door swung open revealing a woman with a large welcoming smile. Tom smiled, too.

"Edith! What a lovely surprise. You look smart as a button. Please, come through."

Maeve O'Reilly was a tall, full-figured woman with a thick salt and pepper braid which she wore over one shoulder. Her taut blouse was pinned in front where it struggled to contain her ample bosom. Her crow's feet spoke of laughter, and the deep creases in her cheeks told of a woman who gave way to smiles.

"This is Tom Clements, and we will assist him to kidnap his fiancée," Edith said with a smirk. "I think James may know where to find her."

"Smashing," Maeve said.

A portly man with winter-white hair appeared from the next room. "A kidnapping? Is that so."

"Tom, this is James and Maeve O'Reilly," Edith said.

Maeve chimed in. "And this strapping young man is Tom Clements."

"Let's have us a wee sit down in the parlor, and you can go on about this scheme of yours," James said.

Maeve turned for her kitchen. "I'll put the kettle on and be back in a tick."

James guided Edith to the parlor, and Tom followed. She peered over her shoulder to ensure the seams of her hose traveled a straight line up the back of her legs.

Edith drew in a breath as they passed a peat burning fire. "There's that lovely turf aroma that says, Ah! Ireland. Who would have thought that so many years of rotting moss and plants would create such a unique scent."

James rolled his eyes. "That's thousands of years and our only source of heat you know."

Tom remembered his mum saying it smelled like wooly hugs and smoked earth.

The parlor was small and sparsely furnished. Edith eased back into a velvet armchair with its nap worn away. She scraped a fingernail back and forth across a tiny rough spot on the armrest, pushed the ottoman out with her foot and nodded to Tom. He sat on the edge and rubbed his hands on his thighs.

Tom noticed James admiring Edith's long, shapely legs as her skirt rose above her knees when she crossed one leg over the other. Tom stifled a chuckle and cleared his throat gaining James's attention just as Maeve appeared with a tray of golden scones spread thick with Devonshire cream and topped with fresh sliced strawberries. She poured black tea from a teapot covered with a hand-knitted cozy.

"Lord knows we could use some liquid wisdom today," Maeve said.

She joined her husband on a deep-buttoned Chesterfield sofa. They all listened intently as Tom explained his dilemma.

James glanced around the room with a lopsided grin. "I know of the Crumlin Road and of the Morrisons. They surely take in single lasses with child and find homes for their wee ones."

He leaned forward, elbows on his knees and rolled his head toward his wife. "You know the Garda will lock us all up if we're caught stealing Mary away."

Maeve and Tom exchanged a look.

"They surely will, but it sounds like that's where we'll find her," Maeve said.

"Aye, Mrs. O'Reilly, but if we're not back before dark, you'll know where to find us," James said.

Maeve slapped her hands on her knees. "Well, I'll leave you to it. Best get a move on before it starts to lash. Sure time waits for no one."

She let out a grunt as James took her arm, and she pushed off with the other.

Tom stood and offered his hand to Edith.

"You catch on quick, Tom Clements."

Edith stood and slipped her arm in his.

"I'll drive since I'm the only one with a motorcar, and I will say that I'm getting quite good at it."

James called over his shoulder. "Are you sure about that?"

"Sure about what?" Edith said.

"The part about you being good at it."

Maeve gave James an impish grin. "You're a cheeky rascal, Mr. O'Reilly."

∼

Tom and James braced themselves as the car jerked forward.

Edith threw her head back and laughed. "That was as smooth as silk."

Within twenty minutes, James pointed to the right. "That's the Crumlin Road ahead. Tom, you best get out here and cut through the woods. Just on the other side, you'll see the house. You can't miss it."

Edith pulled over; Tom got out and faced his friends. "I don't know what to say."

"Did you say your prayers today?" Edith said.

"Indeed, I did."

James nodded. "Good on ya, Lad. We'll see you and Mary back here."

Edith twirled a curl around her finger. "Now remember, James, Love, same first names although I have to say that dropping Sterling for O'Reilly will be a challenge."

"Edith, be serious. Aren't you a wee nervous?"

"I'm a little nervous about getting this Tin Lizzie started without Tom's assistance to turn the crank."

"Aye, I'm not as young as I used to be, so let's just keep it running or there won't be such a thing as a quick getaway if need be."

James nodded toward the trees. "You best get a move on."

As Tom entered the woods, his adrenaline soared at the thought of rescuing Mary. From behind the tree line he heard the bright melody of a skylark singing his song — joyous, clear and fresh.

Chapter 4

The Recovery

When James and Edith arrived at the Morrison's, James got out of the car. Edith remained in the driver's seat with a cheesy smile. James rolled his eyes, walked around the front of the car and opened her door. She swung her legs to the side, took his hand, stepped out, stumbled and fell into his arms. Edith giggled. "Good catch."

A man and woman soon appeared on the porch. Several young girls, most with swollen bellies, congregated along a corner of the house. They were all wearing grey, loose cotton smocks with pinafore coverings of the same.

Edith slid her arm through James's. She walked with a slight limp as they met the couple about half way.

James tipped his cap. "Soft day," James said. "We're the O'Reillys."

A mischievous smile crossed Edith's lips as she nestled in closer to James. "That's James and Edith O'Reilly."

Maintaining a stoic face, James prodded her with his elbow.

"Our young daughter is with child, and we were told that you may be able to help us with our dilemma," Edith said.

The man extended his hand. "You're at the right place. We're the Morrisons."

"Please come in, and I'll put the kettle on," Mrs. Morrison said.

Edith sat down on a tree stump and massaged her ankle. "I seem to have twisted my ankle getting out of the car, and it surely will be too difficult for me to climb the steps."

"Maybe your husband will carry you, and I can tend to it inside."

One of the girls shouted from the porch. "I can't find Mary!"

"She's probably at the back faucet washing up after her gardening. Please collect her for tea," Mrs. Morrison called back.

～

The air was cool, and a stiff breeze kicked up announcing the oncoming rain. A short distance away, the song of a skylark captured Mary's attention. She looked up and saw Tom standing beneath a sycamore's leafy bower. They ran to each other, and he scooped her up in his arms.

Tears welled in her eyes. "Is it really you?"

"You didn't think I'd let you go now, did you?"

Tom got down on one knee and took her hand. "Mary, every bone in me body wants to spend the rest of me life with you. Will you marry me?"

Mary's smile reached for his eyes. "Aye, Tom Clements, I will."

Distant thunder and lightening lit up the sky and it began spitting rain. They sealed the moment with a passionate, unstoppable kiss.

One of the girls rounded the corner of the house. "Well, well, there you are. Looks like your knight in shining armor came for you after all."

"Please, Tom, wait here. I want to speak with her alone."

Mary walked over and searched the girl's eyes for a hint of empathy. "Rebecca, I beg you to say nothing."

Rebecca reached over and lifted the locket from around Mary's neck. "Maybe I will and maybe I won't. What's it worth to you?"

"It's a present from me mum on me eighteenth birthday."

Rebecca smirked and held out her hand. Mary released the clasp and handed it to her.

Rebecca walked away without a word.

～

Tom and Mary darted through the trees. They could hear the sound of Edith's laughter in the distance. Taking short, quick steps, James carried Edith to the car. Mr. Morrison followed with long, heavy strides.

"You won't get away with this!" he called out.

Rebecca stood back grinning and twirling Mary's locket around her neck.

Edith snapped her head around to see Mr. Morrison wasn't far behind. "I was joking about the ankle. Let's hightail it out of here."

She jumped from James's arms and they scurried to the car.

"I'll deal with the likes of you later," James said as Edith scanned the pedals.

Her eyes darted back and forth. "Which pedal is first gear?"

"You're asking me?"

"My mind stalls when I'm under pressure. Let's see, I think it's this one."

The car started to back up.

"Oh, for the love of Mike, Edith."

Edith shifted, working the brake and gas pedals simultaneously. A grinding noise ensued. "I think it's this one. Yes, that's it!"

"Much better," she said easing the brake pedal all the way up and sitting back in her seat.

They circled around by way of a bordering field. She shifted into second gear and they were off.

Edith rested her elbow on the door sill, uttered a snort and laughed with glee. "Pretty fancy footwork, don't you think?"

James drew in a deep breath and blew it out. "Let's get those kids and skedaddle outa here."

Chapter 5

Promising Light

"**They found you,** but first things first. Off with the wellies, and let's get you kids into some dry clothes," Maeve announced.

James smirked. "They wouldn't be soaked through if Edith knew how to get that fancy car of hers moving."

"On the contrary, I didn't see them complaining all cuddled up in the back seat. Isn't that right, Mary?" Edith said.

Mary's cheeks kissed pink.

Tom looked at James and dipped his chin. "I saw you carrying Edith. I thought she might have hurt herself."

Edith winked at Tom. "James witnessed a miraculous recovery."

"Isn't that just grand," James said with a dismissive wave. "Follow me, Tom, and let's see what we can dig up for you to wear."

"I'll get some dry clothes for Mary." Maeve heaved a sigh. "I'm sure they will suit you, dear."

~

They sat down to a feast of leak and potato soup, brown bread and biscuits with fresh creamery butter, along with sliced rosemary lamb and Irish porter cheeses.

"Maeve, you've outdone yourself once again," Edith said. "It's been quite some time since I enjoyed one of your mouth-watering meals."

Mary spooned up a dollop of spicy chutney and spread it on half a biscuit. "Remember the chutney me mum used to make, Tom?" She stopped and pressed her fingers to her lips.

Tom patted her knee. "Aye, I do. You always said she made the best chutney in all of Northern Ireland."

"I'm sure she does," Maeve said and disappeared to the kitchen.

"James was a most renowned sea captain for my husband's fleet. He was Sir Edward's right hand man and earned a commendation for forty years of faithful service," Edith said.

Maeve poked her head in from the kitchen. "As soon as me husband's swelling head returns to normal, we'll take sweets in the sitting room and put a curtain on the day."

~

Vases of brightly colored flowers of all kinds filled the room along with their lovely perfumes. Maeve led them to a window where they viewed her flower gardens drinking up a light drizzle.

Maeve gazed out the window. "Just beyond me roses is where our Anna rests. James built the arbor with scraps of wood from the shipyards. She was so sick for only a wee while and then just dashed short."

"Suppose the good Lord wanted another angel with Him, and Anna was an angel, that one," he said.

The sun set in colored ribbons beyond a sanctuary to hundreds of white and cream roses that threaded themselves twixt and tween the weathered arbor.

Mary caressed her growing belly. "I've never seen anything so beautiful."

~

The next morning, everyone congregated at the breakfast table. Maeve was immersed in her kitchen bustle. "I've rashers and sausages, and how would you like your eggs?"

"Why don't you come on over here for starters so we can discuss the matter at hand," James said.

Maeve wiped her hands on her apron and stood by her husband.

James faced Tom and Mary. "We have three tickets to America. You can have them. Mrs. O'Reilly and I talked it over and no longer have use for them. You can do what you like with the third ticket."

"What Mr. O'Reilly is trying to say is that Anna was with us when we planned to go over, but we've decided to stay put now - to be here with her. At one time these were first class tickets all the way. They were a parting gift from Sir Edward when James retired."

"We missed the scheduled date to use them when Anna fell ill. They're now only good for third class," James said.

"You mean you still have those tickets? I remember the day he gave them to you. It was a God awful mess, an extremely difficult time for all of us." Edith shook her head. "Anna grew up before my very eyes."

James removed an envelope from his trousers and offered it to Tom. "These tickets are for you. Go on, take them; they're your passage to a new life." He cleared his throat. "You'll be placed in the single's quarters, which means you'll be at opposite ends of the ship."

"Isn't there another way?" Tom asked. "I don't want Mary traveling alone."

"I wish there was, but there's not enough time in it to register your marriage, and you would also need your birth certificates."

"The Garda will surely be looking for you," Maeve said.

"The *Cedric* is pulling out in just a few days. You'll have to tie the knot on the other side," Edith said.

James continued. "If I could pull a few strings for you I would, but I don't carry the weight I once did. When you retire, it's like being put out to pasture. Edith, on the other hand, still has influence to get the papers you'll need to board the ship."

A faint smirk played around Edith's lips. "You know me, always an angel of mercy."

Maeve placed her hand on Mary's arm. "The good Lord has seen you this far, and He's not going anywhere."

Edith folded her napkin and set it on the table. "If you will excuse me, I have a lot to do. I will meet you at the docks in plenty of time before your departure. Now, could I gain the assistance of the men to get my Tin Lizzy going?" She chuckled. "I would most likely break my delicate arm turning the crank."

"Who will help you where you're going?" Tom asked.

"Silly you. For a lady of my stature and appeal, there are always men available to help a damsel in distress," Edith said.

"So we'll just have to get there with Mr. O'Reilly's horse and wagon," Maeve said. "I'll say it's a wee better than walking."

Mary could see that Tom was entranced with all Mr. O'Reilly had to say about the journey ahead of them. She kept her gaze fixed on him and studied his face. He didn't ask her how she felt about this decision. She wondered if he felt any misgivings about leaving Ireland.

Maeve took Mary's hand. "Come with me, Lass. I've something I'd like to show you."

They entered a room where an ornate wrought iron bed stood. Sculpted doves adorned a painted white wood dresser and matching vanity. A portrait of a young girl hung on the wall at the far end. She was wearing a powder blue gingham dress which disappeared into a gold gilt gesso frame just below her small waist. Her lips were tinted a soft red, and the girl's dark brown eyes favored Maeve's, like that of a doe, Mary thought.

A large black trunk with dark metal corners and a heavy brass latch sat beneath the portrait. Maeve walked over to the vanity and opened the center drawer where a pale blue linen handkerchief with white tatted trim lay folded in half and in half again. She methodically opened it and disclosed a long, highly polished, ornate brass key. Maeve inserted it into the keyhole, flipped up the latch and slowly raised the lid. Inside, Maeve lifted embroidered linens and towels.

"I bundled me fine crystal and china in their own separate jackets. The wool blankets will assure their safe arrival. They were me mum's," she said with a despondent tone. "I packed them sometime back to pass on to our Anna. I want you to have these and so would me mum."

"Oh, Mrs. O'Reilly, I can't accept these."

"Mr. O'Reilly and I've come to realize we could hang on to these treasures until we die and then what? Memories collecting dust would end up who knows where when we're gone. We want more for Anna's memory."

She looked up at the portrait and then at Mary.

"It's as if we were waiting for you and Tom. What to do with all of this is now clear. You can't put a price on peace of mind."

Maeve handed her the key and walked to the door. "Good night, Lass, sleep well."

"Good night, Mrs. O'Reilly and thank you."

Maeve closed the door behind her.

Chapter 6

Come What May

At Belfast Harbor, Edith appeared through the crowd with Mary's mother.

Edith winked at Tom. "There are just two dairy farms in Ballymena."

Mary threw her arms around her mother's neck. "Oh mum, thank you for being here."

Her mother opened a green satchel and lifted an exquisite white lace veil. She placed it on Mary's head. "I couldn't let you leave without this."

"Thank you. I'll cherish your veil always."

Her mother stepped back and looked on as if taking a mental photograph.

Mary looked at her with downcast eyes. "Didn't dad want to come, too?"

"He wanted to, but one of the cows was calving," she said with a sidelong glance. She looked over Mary's shoulder at Tom. Her eyes softened, and a subtle smile crossed her lips. "We love you both," she whispered.

Edith gave Tom a quick hug and disappeared back into the crowd with Mary's mother.

Maeve turned to her husband. "Let's go home to our flower gardens, Mr. O'Reilly. I've something I'd like to say to me roses."

∿

Raising their eyes up the *Cedric's* massive structure, Tom's wide smile was like sunshine through fresh white linen. "Isn't she grand, Mary?"

Mary felt more trepidation and less excitement than Tom. Her eyes flashed with uncertainty as she caressed her belly bump.

Tom lifted her chin and looked into her eyes. "You're going to be safe. I won't let anything happen to you or our wee baby."

The throng of various languages and dialects added to the sense of chaos as the ship was readied for the voyage. A medical examination of the third-class passengers consisted of a brief glance into their eyes for signs of trachoma followed by a check for typhoid and lice. The first-class and second-class passengers merely presented papers from their doctors. Tom handed over the papers Edith had given him. Mary breathed a sigh of relief as they were urged to advance.

Scanning fore and aft along the portside of the ship, dozens of ropes, as thick as a sailor's arm, moored the boat to the quay. A forward ramp leading to the A and B decks allowed the first-class patrons to board separately.

Mary admired refined ladies dressed in lavish, high fashion clothing with bustles and ruffles and hand beading, wide-brimmed hats trimmed with felt and snowy egret feathers. They promenaded up the plank beyond the crowds of tattered and torn. A small army hustled luggage and supplies onto the ship, and Mary wondered if the delicate cargo in her trunk would arrive undamaged.

Mary jumped to a sharp, abrupt voice erupting from the mass of frightened and confused emigrants. A woman with a Cavan Irish accent emerged. She was holding a rosary.

"There's more people standing on the dock than in me village, and this is only Belfast. I wonder what the pier looks like on the other side," she said with a husky voice.

She wore dingy khaki trousers and an oversized grey flannel shirt which was cinched around her thick middle with a wide leather belt. She sported a small porter's cap with a feather along one side from some bird Mary couldn't name. Mary's eyes lit up with curiosity at this woman displaying cavernous dimples embedded in her plump cheeks.

"Cousin Moss is giving me Donnie a job at the steel mill where he works. Moss does the hiring and firing there."

She rested both hands on her hips and opened her feet to take a wider stance. "I'll be over when Donnie has the money to send for me, and we're going to tie the knot at St. James Roman Catholic Church. I'm Gracey and here he comes now."

Gracey jutted her chin in Tom's direction. "Since me cousin, Moss, is the foreman, maybe he can help you. That's if you don't already have a job waiting when you get there, which I doubt you do. It's not easy for us foreigners to find work," she babbled on. "Too many going over all the time. The way I see it, you have to grab life by the throat and shake it."

The man stretched his neck out. "There you go again yammering away at people you don't even know."

He swung his arm around and gave Gracey an affectionate whack on her behind. "She's a big noise, that one," he chuckled.

The dockside dealmaking was fast and furious. Tom saw pound notes changing hands and arrangements being made. People leveraged what they had in exchange for some hope on the other side.

Tom raised his finger. "Wait! I've an extra ticket. I want nothing more, nothing less than a chance to work at your cousin's steel mill."

Donnie raked his fingers through his scraggly beard. "Mmmm, I don't know. I told a bloke from the Lyon's Pub I'd talk to Moss for him."

Gracey poked Donnie and narrowed her eyes.

"Ok, ok, it's a bargain," Donnie said.

Tom handed him the ticket, and they shook hands.

Gracey smiled widely exposing a mouth full of uneven, yellow-stained horsey teeth.

To Mary, it was the most beautiful smile she had ever seen.

Hundreds stood by to bid bon voyage to the departing. Tears swept across the faces of those leaving their loved ones behind. Most passengers were on a common mission to escape from poverty, to find better housing and occupations to support their families. Tom and Mary were from the North. Their purpose was not the same, but what hardships awaited them were equally unpredictable, and Mary wondered if they, too, would ever see their families again.

She stood on her tiptoes and whispered in Tom's ear. "That lad over there is surely not well enough for such a journey as this."

A man held a small boy's limp body in one arm while the other curled around a woman's shoulders. Her eyes were pink, lids sagging, and her face hung loose and long. Mary wondered if more of these men and women looked older than they really were.

"His dad'll take care of him," Tom answered with a stiff upper lip.

Mary felt the distress in the woman's eyes, and she wondered if the boy would likely be turned away or worse, not see the end of their voyage. Our baby's life is just beginning, she thought.

The passengers congregated along the upper deck. A man shouted through a megaphone. "All passengers please make your way to your assigned quarters. The *Cedric* is ready to ship out!"

Mary's pulse raced, but she knew she had to be strong for her own sake and for the precious cargo growing inside her. A light drizzle fell as the quartermaster sounded the departing blast. The time of separation was upon Tom and Mary once again. A cloud billowed across the sky bringing with it a distant rumble of thunder as they held a soft, lingering kiss.

Gracey extended her hand. "We got to get on with it, Lass."

Before Tom and Donnie joined the men at the back of the ship, they stood and watched Mary and Gracey shuffle along with the other single women toward the bow.

Mary stopped at the top of the stairs and looked for Tom but he had disappeared below.

She took hold of the icy metal handrail, turned and scanned the crowd gathered along the pier. Rolling grey clouds blew over the tops of colorful harbor buildings. In the distance, Edith and her mum looked on from the red Model T.

Chapter 7

The Journey

Uncertain of which way to turn, Mary looked at Gracey who had established herself as fearless and responsible.

"Well, it's everything I expected and then some." Gracey surveyed the vessel. "Come with me."

They trooped slowly down the narrow steel stairs into the crush of an entrance hall and through dark doorways, no more than a part of a moving mass, Mary thought. She cringed at the rising dank, salty air. Looking around, she wanted to run back out.

They entered through a heavy steel portal where fifty women were fighting for forty beds. The iron framed berths supported mattresses filled with straw or dried seaweed. Gracey clutched Mary's hand, and they waded through a sea of confused, rambunctious women.

"I didn't know a ship could groan so much. Didn't hear it up on top," Gracey said. "Sure the first-class folks won't be losing sleep, God knows."

A bitter, sour taste of half-digested food jumped up in Mary's throat. She felt compelled to vomit but managed to force it back down.

"It looks like we're a bit late for the dance," Gracey muttered. "I had no clue we'd be fighting with these tinkers and knackers for a bed."

"What are we going to do?" Mary asked, looking more pallid by the minute.

Gracey pressed her forefinger to her chin, and a mischievous smile crossed her lips. "I've got it covered, Mary. Be back in a tic."

"What's clattering about in that brain of yours, Gracey?"

"You just watch this," she said with a snigger.

Mary noticed at least a dozen women with protruding bellies and large breasts indicating there were more of them with child than she would have imagined.

Gracey removed the feather from her cap, adjusted it to a jauntier angle and marched to the center of the room. "Now hear this, ladies. I've been assigned to assist the matron with her duties, and it's the captain's orders that all women with child and elderly ladies be given a proper bed. The rest of you lot will grab a hammock and hang it along the walls." She plopped down on a bed. "Sure this one's for me."

One of the women spoke up. "Are you to be down here the whole trip with us?"

"I'll be sticking around to keep me eyes open to the goings on down here, which I might add is also the captain's orders. And what is your name, Lass?"

The woman stopped in front of Mary and scoffed, "It's Thelma and you best stay out of me way."

"Pay her no mind," Gracey said. "She's talking a load of Blarney."

Mary looked straight at Thelma. "You best be off before the banshees carry you away."

"Good on ya, Mary," Gracey said.

One of the women pointed above. "Hey, Thelma, here they come!"

Thelma crouched down, her eyes darting around the room. The women let out a laugh and Thelma's face reddened. "Bugger off!"

"Now Thelma, they're just funnin' ya," Gracey said.

～

At the stern, Tom battled with thoughts such as if he hadn't met Edith and the O'Reilly's, he and Mary might have settled somewhere in Ireland. Reconciling with their families in the future would have been a possibility, but it was too late to turn back. Tom remembered his promise to Mary, that little voice chanting in his mind. *You're going to be safe; I won't let anything happen to you or our wee baby.*

Tom passed by a porthole and stopped to see a distant ship approaching Belfast Harbor. As he felt the *Cedric* increase the distance between them and the patina dome of Belfast City Hall, a harmonica began to play softly. A lively fiddle joined in raising everyone's spirits and soon toes were tapping. It wasn't long before their gloomy surroundings were abound with a full-blown ceilidh. Men gyrated to the Irish music regardless of their nationality.

"How do we get our dance partners here?" a man asked.

"Ah, we'll figure that out when the time is at hand," Donnie said. He raised his chin. "Those blokes over there smuggled about one hundred bottles of stout and nearly that many packs of fags on board. They'll be cleaning up before we hit the Statue of Liberty. Sure it's the blackest of markets."

Donnie brought back three pints, popped the cap off one, guzzled it down without taking a breath and let out a belch.

"Here, this one's for you." He shrugged.

They sat on the floor with the dark stuff and surveyed the goings on.

A crew member entered the room, grabbed a bottle for himself and took a long hard swig.

Donnie tossed a coin into the crate and helped himself to another. "What's the situation with our women?"

The man waved him off. "Listen up everyone. Now that you blokes are all settled in, I'm going to go over the captain's expectations of you for the voyage."

He emptied the bottle with a couple more gulps.

"While we're at sea, as you might expect, the first-class passengers and fares they pay are what keep this vessel afloat. Although you paid a few bob here, you are to be considered not much more than ballast. You go up only when the salon passengers are taking their meals. The rest of the time you're to be in these quarters or at your assigned work detail. No one is to be on the deck after midnight. If for any reason anyone has a problem with this, you'll be taking a swim. Any questions?"

Tom raised an eyebrow. "I'd say he's a fella to be reckoned with."

Chapter 8

Holding On

Similar events were going on in the single women's quarters with one subtle difference. The women's matron entered the room clapping her hands.

"Everyone stop with your clatter."

Gracey stepped forward after recognizing the matron's mission.

"Excuse me, but before you begin with your announcements, I want to inform you that there's quite a few Gaelic speakers here, and I'd be happy to translate."

The matron gave Gracey a skeptical nod and resumed explaining the protocols. Mary noticed some of the ladies stifle a giggle.

Her mission accomplished, Gracey brushed her hands and joined the others.

Mary lay on her bed and propped herself up on her elbows. "That's gas, Gracey. You have a lovely get-up-and-go about you. Do you really speak Gaelic?"

"Not a word," she said from the corner of her mouth. "But it looks like those who do, seem to find me jocular gibberish quite amusing. By the way, you look mighty peaky, Mary. How far along are you, Lass?"

"About four months."

"So we're nearly half way there. The sea is calm now. Rest while you can, and I'll get the lay of the land in the meantime. I'll be just a spitting distance away." Gracey paused, "I'm happy we met, Mary. It'll surely give me purpose to pass the hours and days ahead."

∾

Early that evening, the matron and Gracey appeared on the deck followed by a slew of boisterous women. Tom scanned the crowd looking for Mary.

"Tell those women to move ahead and make room for the others," the matron instructed Gracey.

Along with her Gaelic nonsense, Gracey pointed the way.

Donnie walked up and tapped her on the shoulder. "Are you daft? What are you doing, woman?"

"Gaining respect as a crew member."

"A crew member? Why in the name of God would you do that?"

"To get Mary and me beds and now here I am stuck playing a buffoon until we hit New York. But at the end of the day, I'm number two in the women's quarters which is quite a feat, if I do say so meself."

Tom stepped up to Gracey. "Where's Mary?"

"She'll be up with Thelma straight away."

Turning to Donnie and Tom she cackled, "Now why don't one of you two shiftless Irishmen go collect her before I report you to the captain. I'll meet you back here in two shakes." Gracey swiftly continued across the deck.

"Brilliant, just brilliant," Donnie said shaking his head.

Tom breathed a sigh of relief when Mary came into view. He hugged her then held her at arm's length. "Mary, you look so pale. How do you feel?"

"I'm just a wee queazy in that stale air down there, but a woman from Larne is well stocked with digestive biscuits which helps me to feel better."

She looked up at him and forced a smile. "It's so grand to be with you up here. I'll be right as rain in no time. Sure the journey has just begun, and I'll find me sea legs in short order."

The signal soon sounded for them to return to their quarters. Tom looked up at the sky full of stars — beacons of hope, he thought. The big buttery moon passed through cirrus clouds on their first night at sea. Tom saw the angst in her soft brown eyes. He held her close and kissed her hair.

∾

When Tom went below, he spotted one of the younger lads rummaging through his gear. He was soon joined by a leathery-face, heavy-built man with wide, full lips that drew back to a snarl. Tom knew they were Catholics for he'd seen them sign the cross over themselves and glare at him upon the ship's departure.

The man swaggered over to him and stood just inches away. Tom felt his hot, foul breath on his face. Tom clenched his fists, his arms remaining at his sides.

"Well look what the cat dragged in."

The lad jumped in. "We'd inform you of your rights, but you have none, you no good git. Right, Sean?"

Donnie took a long, hard swallow, wiped his mouth across his sleeve and called out, "I'll put five pounds on the Prot!"

Another man raised his index finger, "I'll take that bet on Sean!"

They all joined in throwing their pound notes down on the winner. Tom could hear that Sean was the favorite by far.

Sean grabbed Tom's shirt and shoved him against the ship's steel wall. "We know you're not Catholic. You even stink like a Prot."

The lad stepped closer. "God save the Queen, aye mate? And just where's she now when you need her?"

Tom lunged forward and launched a pointed jab to Sean's jaw. Sean's head thrust back, and his bottom teeth cut into his upper lip splitting it almost in half. Blood squirted from the wound and down Sean's chin. Sean charged Tom delivering a head-butt causing Tom to temporarily lose his senses.

Everyone moved further back. Tom threw three more sharp jabs to Sean's mid-section and he went down. Sean got up and hurled a haymaker to Tom's ribs. Tom felt a deep pain in his lungs.

The men cheered as they threw their own feint punches in the air. Donnie spun around, fell against the wall and to the floor. "I'll have me another!"

With fire in his eyes, Tom threw four more upper cuts to Sean's gut. Tom knew when he launched his final blows, Sean would not be getting up.

Donnie let out a whoop, jumped up and gathered up his winnings. Several men waved with disgust, and they all returned to their hobnobbing.

Tom squeezed his swollen eyes with a scowl. He tweaked his nose. Blood streamed from his nostrils.

Donnie joined Tom and handed him a rag. "Jaysus, Tom, are you ever a mess. He broke your nose, ya know."

Pain shot throughout Tom's hand, which he saw was becoming a marriage of blue and green. He turned his head and spit blood. "What the hell was that all about, and who are those louts?"

"I think they might've been sent by a bloke from me hometown who figured I'd get him a job at the steel mill with Moss." Donnie sheepishly rolled his eyes upward. "I might've said something about it over some pub talk, probably one of me times of idiocy. I suppose he heard about our dealmaking at the docks and sent those gobshites to break your arm. You can't work with a broken arm."

Tom walked over to Sean who was sitting bent over on the floor. He raised his head when Tom crouched down across from him. "You go tell your boss to come and deal with me himself next time."

Tom looked around the room then back at Donnie. "You see him anywhere, Donnie?"

"If I were you, I'd quit while you're ahead."

Chapter 9

The Sea Drank The Cradle

Gracey woke to Mary's whimpers and discovered her shaking and sweating profusely. "You're hot with fever, Lass."

A sharp pain hit deep in Mary's bowels as a wave of nausea swept over her. "I'm needing a bucket," she said with a brittle whisper.

Gracey set the bucket on the floor and helped Mary to roll on her side. She cradled Mary's stomach and supported her forehead as Mary began to vomit copiously.

Thelma emerged with a wet cloth and cup of water. "Here, take this for she's dehydrating mighty fast."

Gracey held the cup to Mary's mouth. She took a sip then began to shudder. Mary vomited a sour bile followed by dry heaves that caused her to barely be able to catch her breath. Thelma dabbed her brow while Gracey tended to the bucket. Mary fell into a deep, dreamless sleep.

~

Just before dawn, Mary's eyes flew open, and she let out a hurdling screech.

"Look, Gracey," Thelma said. She tipped her head and nodded to a growing bright red pool drowning the mattress under Mary. Mary looked up at Gracey and they locked eyes, their hearts beating erratically.

"We need more towels, blankets, anything," Gracey implored. Only a few women appeared with whatever they would sacrifice.

When it was over, Gracey sat next to Mary holding a silent bundle in the crook of her arm. Barely responsive, Mary closed her eyes and turned her head to the side.

Tears clogged Gracey's throat. "I'll tend to your wee one."

She stood and turned to Thelma. "It'll soon be time for us to go up, and I need to find Tom straight away. Will you stay with Mary?"

"Aye, I will, but you know I need me some fresh air."

I'll be back in time; you have me word."

Mary moaned in Thelma's arms.

~

The air was heavy with humidity that wouldn't quite turn into rain. Tom and Donnie waited on deck with watchful eyes for the women to appear. Gracey was without Mary. She quickly bypassed Donnie and continued directly to Tom. His heart raced as she looked into his eyes, tears filming her own.

Her chin quivered as her eyes glistened with pooling tears. "Mary lost the baby this morning. I'm so sorry, Tom."

Tom's eyes widened. "What about Mary? I need to go to her."

He turned toward the steps, and Gracey grasped his arm.

"You can't go down there, Tom. We'll help her to be up here tonight, and I need you to listen for what I have to say." She took a deep breath. "We won't be docking for several days, so I suggest we give your son a proper burial at sea. Once Mary is with you, I'll slide the wee bundle through the rear porthole. And I think it proper that Father Flanagan give a blessing no matter your religion. He's the only man of the cloth on this ship."

Tom's eyes took on a hollow quality.

"Did you hear me, Tom? Will you be here at half twelve?"

Tom nodded and spoke with a labored, raspy undertone. "Aye, I'll be here."

"Alright then. I have to go now." Gracey patted him on the back and walked over to Donnie. "Go on now and fetch Father Flanagan."

～

Tom, Donnie and Father Flanagan appeared at the rail.

"Tom, I know what you're going through. Gracey and I went through this not so long ago." Donnie took a deep breath and blew out his cheeks. "I was just at the pub with me lads for a pint, and well, I wasn't with her."

He stepped back as Gracey and Mary came into view. Tom helped Mary to the rail and wrapped his arm around her shoulders.

Father Flanagan raised his right hand, signed the cross and prayed. "Lord, God, ever caring and gentle, we commit to your love this wee one, quickened to life for so short a time. Enfold him in eternal life. We pray for his parents who are saddened by the loss of their child. Give them courage and help them in their pain and grief. May they all meet one day in the joy and peace of your kingdom. We ask this through Christ our Lord. Amen."

The wind soon transformed still waters into choppy, ferocious waves. Tom felt an unforgiving anger sweep across him as he removed his coat and covered Mary.

Gracey slid the bundle through a porthole and into the churning black sea.

Father Flannigan's voice escalated as if he were calling out to God. "Be mindful of our brothers and sisters who have fallen asleep in the peace of Christ and all the dead who have faith only you can know. Lead them to the fullness of the resurrection and gladden them with your light. Amen."

He laid his hand on Tom's shoulder. "I thought it best to baptize him, too. There's a reason the good Lord took your wee baby to be with Him. Far be it from me to know, but God's ways are wise."

Tom couldn't recall what Father Flanagan said to him as the priest walked away.

He corralled Mary in his arms. She buried her face in his chest and broke into hard racking cries.

The rain moved toward them like a wrath's veil of sorrow. The distant sky was ablaze with lightening, and the rain lashed Tom's face. The sea seemed to throb grey with woe. When his baby went under that final wave, time seemed suspended.

Tom and Mary stood in a thick, pervasive grief that had settled upon them like a heavy-laden fog. The pain that flowed was as palpable as the frigid waters below. There would be no grave.

They remained entwined as the storm passed, the sea calmed and the moon shone discreetly from behind cloudy skies.

He'll be alone in the cold, dark water, she thought. Was me baby yanked down into nothingness? Would he have lived if I'd taken better care of meself? Was this God's wrath for our sins?

Mary watched a small wave shimmer. It was just enough for her to witness these last few precious moments. The steamship's foghorn echoed across the water bringing an abrupt end to the rituals.

~

Each day ran into the next. Mary spent most of her time in bed, her body mending, and she wondered if she would ever find any peace in her life again. How many days had passed? Mary couldn't be sure. She would, however, always remember when someone shouted, *"There she is!"*

A throng of passengers clamored to the top deck. The first-class passengers dropped their breakfast utensils and raced to the rail. Tom, Mary, Donnie and Gracey huddled at the bow. Wearing a halo of spiked rays, the Statue of Liberty held a flaming torch high above her head.

The passengers uncorked both champagne and porter. Clinking bottles and the tinkle of glass on glass, as well as rousing cheers, rang out in celebration. You could touch the excitement with your hand. Their journey was over. They had arrived in America.

Mary looked up at Tom with vacant eyes. Massive cement formations had replaced the majestic cliffs and green meadows of home.

Word quickly spread that they'd be docking within three hours and everyone should prepare accordingly.

Banners unfurled and hundreds of people greeted the *Cedric*. In exactly nine arduous days, their ship from Belfast Harbor had arrived at White Star pier 48 in New York City.

Tom, Mary and their friends joined the third-class passengers onto a barge for Ellis Island where they were to be processed.

Mary found herself passing into a massive red brick structure known as the immigration inspection station. Tom reached for her hand. Mary gave a weak smile. It was a bittersweet beginning.

Chapter 10

O' America

"Names?" asked a man behind the counter with a heavy Dublin accent.

"Thomas Hugh Clements and Mary Clements," Tom said.

"Well, the ship's manifest here doesn't show you're married," the man retorted.

Tom stood firm. "We're soon to be married."

"Well, you'll make me job a hell of a lot easier if you are. So why the hell do you have the same last name?"

"There's a reason for that," Tom said sharply.

"Aye, so she's up the poll, is she?"

"Look, let's get on with this," Tom said.

The man looked over at Donnie and Gracey.

"Are these two gits with you?"

"We are," Gracey said. "And do you have a first name, Mr. Mallory?"

"Just what the name tag says."

"Back off, Your Grace," Donnie said.

She gave Donnie a shrug and looked over at Mary. "Touchy, isn't he?"

Mallory reached under the counter, pulled up a piece of paper, tore off a strip and began writing.

"I'll let you through so you can get hitched, married or otherwise entangled across from here. I'll give you the right papers, but it'll cost you." He lifted his eyebrows. "Let's take a look inside that trunk of yours."

Tom nodded to Mary. "Do what the man says, Mary."

Mary pulled out an embroidered handkerchief from her satchel. She unfolded it exposing the key and handed it to Tom. He opened the trunk. Her mother's wedding veil lay across the top. Tom lifted it up and handed it to Mary.

"I'm not interested in that. Let's see what else is in there."

Tom nudged Mary, and she revealed a silver creamer and sugar set.

"That'll do for starters. And what's in that blanket there? Our friend, the Justice of the Peace, is a greedy sort."

Mary glared at the man with narrowed eyes. "Tom, it's Mrs. O'Reilly's porcelain teapot. She'd really want us to have that."

Mallory opened the blanket further. "Teapot or marriage certificate. What's it going to be? Take this to Magistrate Williams, and he'll take care of you."

Tom leveled his gaze at her. "Do what he says, Mary. I'll replace them tenfold."

"But Tom…" Mary glared at the man, a muscle working in her jaw.

I've left me family, me baby is dead and now this. What's next, she thought.

Mallory peered at Donnie. "Can I interest you in a similar offer?"

"No, thanks," Gracey said. "We're getting hitched at St. James Roman Catholic Church. Just needed to get us both on American soil, and thanks to Tom and Mary, we're on our way." Gracey flashed him a cavity-riddled smile.

"Mind your way through those streets. They can be a treacherous lot out there," Mallory cackled. "You might leave me the key for safekeeping at that."

"You won't be needing it," Tom said. He slid the key into his front pocket, and they began walking to where Mallory had indicated, leaving Donnie and Gracey to mind the trunk.

Weaving through the crowd, Tom and Mary saw scores of makeshift tables and booths with moneychangers and boarding house proprietors. Men wearing top hats and finely trimmed beards peddled goods and services of all types.

Tom gravitated to one such booth where a sign read:

Marriage Certificates
Frank Williams,
Justice of the Peace

Tom handed Williams the note, and he glanced quickly over its contents.

"Is it true you can marry us this minute?"

"So Mallory sent you. Seems he has quite a few of you Irish ghouls coming in today."

"Can we get on with this?" Tom asked.

"And in what form will your payment be?"

Mary unfolded her veil and produced Maeve's teapot.

"That will do nicely if you throw in that pretty lace veil. My Mrs. would like to have that."

Mary stepped back and was quick to answer, "I'll not part with this."

She placed it on her head and held a firm stance.

Williams snickered and gave Tom their marriage certificate. "Better head right back. Mallory won't want to miss his five o'clock standing at his favorite watering hole."

～

"There they are, no worse for wear," Donnie quipped. "Sure she'll be streaming out orders to him in no time. Tom, get your notepad ready," he chortled on.

"Let's go find cousin Moss at the so-called kissing post," Gracey said. "It's where everybody meets their relatives you know."

"They say it's the last stop before a new beginning for everyone," Donnie said. "Now, what did you say he looked like, Your Grace?"

"A big pink pig with a heap of red hair. I heard that if his wife Angela's with him, he'll have a ring in his nose, to be sure. She's a door full of woman to boot, so mind your manners."

Donnie extended an arm across the front of the group.

"That wouldn't be him, would it now?"

Moss had broad beefy shoulders and a thick slab of a torso. Lots of fiery red hair tossed about every which way.

"He's a mountain of a man, he is. Didn't I tell you?" Gracey gave Donnie a quick jab with her elbow.

"And it looks like he's without his overseer," Donnie said.

Gracey called out to Moss. "We're over here you beast of a man!" She reached up, patted his face and introductions were made.

"First things first. Let's have us a pint," Moss said.

Chapter 11

By Your Side

"Pints all around," roared Moss. "I've got me a terrible thirst."

The bartender began pulling the five pints of foamy black Guinness. Mary noticed a white-haired man with a purple bulbous nose leaning against the bar. His hands trembled as he raised a pint to his lips.

Mary lowered her gaze, turned her face away from Moss and looked up at Tom. Her eyes glistened. "I'll have me a fizzy, if you don't mind."

Gracey prodded, "Oh, go on, you've earned a pint. Donnie'll slurp up what you don't finish."

Tom leaned into Mary, took her hand and gave it a gentle squeeze. "We need to take what he offers, Mary."

"Make up your minds, ladies," Moss said. "Your man here doesn't have all day. There's tongues hanging down all along the bar."

"Make mine a pint," Mary said flatly.

"Good on ya, girl," Moss said. "I was spot on from the beginning, now wasn't I?"

Mary looked at Tom with a blank stare and swallowed a smile.

Moss raised his glass to eye level. "Welcome to America! Uncle Sam's glad you're here, and Mother Ireland's glad you're gone."

Mary remained silent as the others raised their glasses high. "Slainte," Gracey said.

Moss surveyed the group. "I've been here ten years, and I know the lay of the land. I'm starting to rise up the ladder at Marcey Foundry. I also have me own tenements and laundry business. The first eight years here I helped every Paddy, Mick and Mary coming off the boat to get settled into their new surroundings. I'd help these Irish get places to live and even put them up in me own gaff only to see them betray me and align themselves with mobsters, ne'er-do-wells and moneylenders."

"Me cousin's just blowing hot air," Gracey teased.

Moss gave a short, mirthless laugh. "I meant well helping me own people, but I also learned the hard way about those who can't be trusted." He leaned forward. "We need to stick together. For starters, I saw you shoot down a whiskey around the corner of the bar, Donnie." Moss gave him a cold stare. "You'll get yourself fired if you have a problem with the drink."

Moss pressed on. "I don't work for free anymore, and I've learned well that I need to protect the things that I call mine. I'll help you out for starters if you're willing to do what I say. I know you all need work and a place to stay; neither of these are easy feats just off the boat. This city is crawling with slumlords and sweatshops, not to mention crooked cops and politicians. The sooner you understand this, the better. You're up against the Italians, the Jews and Poles as well. They're all wanting the same as you."

Tom studied Moss's face as he tried to discern whether these were scare tactics or the true lay of the land. He knew America was not really "the land of milk and honey" as so many immigrants thought it to be, but he had not heard of graft and greed to this extent. Tom briefly wished he was back in Ballymena discussing ways to outwit a farmer at the local cattle auction.

Moss finished his pint. "Same again if you will, good man."

He waved his finger in the air then set out the rules of engagement. "Donnie and Tom will start at the foundry Monday morning at six. It's a grueling twelve-hour shift that'll sweat the life out of you if you don't drink lots of water. I'll be watching over the whole lot of you, and I'll have no trouble replacing anyone who doesn't carry their weight, which also goes for the ladies."

Mary noticed a rat scurry across the far end of the room.

Moss struggled to run his fingers through his tangled, dense mop. "There's a boat from Cork due in tomorrow at noon, so I suggest you take what I'm offering".

He peered at Tom and Donnie. They nodded in agreement.

"Angela runs a laundry at the flats, and it's chopping right along with all the police and firemen uniforms we have coming in. We weren't expecting either of you ladies, but it looks like this just might work out. You'll help Angela with the washing, ironing and mending. It's all done in the cellar, and there's more money to be had in the ironing if it passes her inspection."

"So long as we don't have to wear a nose ring," Gracey said.

Mary covered her mouth with her hand and stifled a giggle.

"Just do as you're told, and she'll keep you on. I'll pick up the laundry with me pushcart, and we can turn these uniforms around faster now with the three of you."

"Tom, you and Mary will stay in the cellar until something else opens up in one of the flats. The floors are wet down there and sure no better than those in Limerick."

"Aye, but the difference is in Limerick the die is cast. Their fate is sealed. Here, you can get up and out of the squalor," Donnie said.

Moss stood and looked over the group. "So, if this suits everyone, we'll head out for the flats."

They loaded their belongings onto Moss's pushcart and walked a full hour to the Lower East Side of Manhattan.

∿

"The lord of the realm has returned to his manor house," Moss announced. His jocular manner spread a prideful grin across his face. "Tom, might you push me cart the rest of the way?"

Tom took the handle and Moss walked ahead of the group. A small band of men congregated beyond a courtyard. They hushed as Moss walked toward them. A large woman appeared at the arched opening and approached him. Moss stood in front of her and seemed to be giving a debriefing as her eyes wandered around his massive body, eyeing Gracey and Mary.

She walked over to Gracey. "You look just like you do in the family photos, only older," she said. "I'm Angela."

Gracey returned a crisp little laugh. "And you aren't as beastly looking as I was told. I'm Gracey."

Angela puffed out her bottom lip. "Have you eaten or did Moss figure a couple of pints would do the trick?"

"I'm starving," Gracey said.

"I'll rummage up some meat sandwiches when I get a chance," Angela said.

"Angela, take Donnie and Gracey upstairs. I'll show Tom and Mary where they're staying. We'll hook back up later."

Moss stroked his bristly jawline. "I've also got a few knots to untie with those restless inhabitants who greeted me. I might be able to come up with some part-time work for a few of them." He turned to Donnie and Tom. A small smile flickered across his lips. "They don't have the connections you do."

Moss ushered Tom and Mary down to a damp, musty cellar. They stood before a twelve foot square concrete room with only a small window along the outside wall just inches from the ceiling. It let in no more than eight square inches of light illuminating a patch of what looked to be algae on the floor.

"I'll see that a mattress is carried down before tonight," Moss said. "There's some matches on the ledge behind the lantern and cleaning supplies around the corner."

"Excuse me. Where might I find the loo?" Mary asked.

"There's one on each floor up the stairs. But you two have your very own down here. The choice is yours." Moss chortled and disappeared at the top.

Tom and Mary heard constant dripping as they surveyed their surroundings.

"My God, Tom, what is this place?"

"It looks to be an old coal room."

Tom promptly set the kerosene lamp ablaze further illuminating the space and revealing a water-stained concrete floor. Dried mud and unknown debris oozed from several cracks. A leaky spigot connected to a hose which snaked around the corner, and a chamber pot sat next to it.

"There's the toilet you're looking for Mary, and that's where the dripping is coming from."

"I'll be needing some disinfectant to get rid of the mold and mildew down here," she said.

He spit in each hand, winked at her and tightened the connection with one quick turn.

"Looks like all that hard work on the farm paid off," she said. "Let's pull the wee table and chairs to the middle. I'll find some rags and spiff up this kip of a joint."

Tom found a couple of loose concrete slabs and placed them under each end of the trunk raising it off the floor.

"I'm going to see where the other end of this hose might be," he said.

Mary scrubbed the table and chairs, removed a blue linen tablecloth from the trunk and snapped it into place. Two mono-grammed white linen napkins brought to mind her memories of the O'Reillys who were monogrammed on her heart.

"I like what you've done, but don't grow too fond of this place," Tom said as he rounded the corner.

"Don't you fret. We're planting no roots here, to be sure," she said.

Tom wiggled his finger for her to join him. "I found the end of the hose. Would you like to see your new place of employment?"

He held the lantern up, and Mary followed him to another corner of the cellar. The light exposed three large iron tubs perched above a single grate which was high enough for a small fire beneath it.

"That's how you get hot water in a cold-water flat," Tom said.

She shrugged. "It's late, and you surely must be as hungry as I am. Let's see to Angela's sandwiches."

Mary wondered what the meat might be in this shanty part of town but then decided maybe it's best she not know.

Chapter 12

Longing

Come Monday morning, Tom rapped on Donnie's door.

"Donnie boy, you best get moving if you fancy your job." He knocked again.

Gracey opened the door and plopped Donnie's cap on his head as he fumbled with his suspenders.

She took a deep breath and blew it out through her mouth. "He's all yours. Three days of it and still in the drink."

She shook her head at Donnie and slid past him. "Me job is waiting."

Tom's eyes narrowed as he waved a hand in front of his face. "Don't breathe near Moss or you'll be bidding good day to this job, cousin or no cousin."

Angela waited in the basement with Mary, and the men followed Gracey down just as Moss appeared. His red hair caught the overhead light. It shined like bright copper, Mary thought.

"I'll take Donnie and Tom to the foundry then pick up the uniforms," Moss said. "Ladies, it's time to light a fire and get the kettles boiling. Angela will take you across the alleyway where you'll gather wood from the scrap pile."

"You'll start the mending as soon as we get back. We'll share our food until your first pay, and I'll figure out what I'm owed. After that, you're on your own," Angela said.

Gracey tapped her chin with her forefinger and rolled her eyes. "So what do we do in our spare time?"

Mary looked away and laughed to herself.

Angela handed each of the men a brown paper bag. "It's potluck until then."

Tom gave Mary a kiss on the cheek and guided Donnie up the stairs behind Moss.

"All the best, Lads, and keep your wits about you," Gracey said.

"Ladies, let's first have us some tea and a bun before we get down to it," Angela said.

~

Mary held her palms up. "Month after month of the same thing, day in and day out. Me hands are so burned and blistered from stirring these pots, Gracey."

Mary swept away wet, loose strands of hair from her face with her forearm. "Is it always going to be like this?"

"I'm afraid this is it, dearie."

"So why doesn't Angela ever work with us down here?"

Gracey cocked her head back and snickered. "Why should she? She's got us, and I heard Moss say he's hiring even more of us foreigners. 'Business is booming,' he said."

Angela appeared at the top of the stairs. "There's a letter here addressed to Tom Clements. It has Irish post. Any takers?"

Mary set down the uniform she was working on and hastened up the steps.

"Looks like this finally found you two," Gracey said.

"It's from Tom's mum and dad, to be sure. Tom wrote to them a while back. He told them where we are and also told them about the fate of our baby." She looked away.

Gracey reached inside her blouse, pulled out a bunched up hankie and handed it to Mary. "Maybe you best sit down, Lass."

Mary tucked the letter in her skirt pocket, blotted away a few stray tears, and they returned to their chairs. Mary reached for the uniform and continued her task.

Gracey blinked hard. "Are you daft? Open it Mary; the mending can wait."

Mary inspected the envelope and thought of the voyage it also took to reach America. It was tattered and badly stained as one might expect — a small price to pay in comparison to the voyage she and Tom endured.

Gracey scrunched her face. "Glory be, go ahead and open it. Besides, it's indeed about you, too."

Mary raised the envelope to the light. "No, Tom will be the one to open it. Besides, quitting time is nearly here."

Mary tucked it back in her pocket, stood up and disappeared into the coal room. She returned dressed in her long, olive green wool coat, plaid tartan scarf and gloves.

"And just where do you think you're going?"

"I'm going to meet Tom at the foundry. It's only a few blocks, and I have to show this to him straight away. Won't you go with me and surprise Donnie?"

"What? And put a damper on his shenanigans? Sure he'll be heading to Kilcullen's."

Gracey hung her head, and then just as quickly, she sat rigid as a block of stone. "It's not safe for a woman to be walking these streets alone at night."

"I'll be fit and well; don't you worry now."

"Do wait for Tom to come home, won't you, Mary?"

"We'll be back in short order."

∾

Mary stowed the letter in her coat pocket and hurried through the dark, frigid streets. Massive warehouses and scattered trees, bare of leaves, seemed frozen against the black sky. The wind picked up and felt angry to her, growing stronger and whipping her face. She knotted her scarf tighter and tucked her gloved hands under her arms. Mary stood under a street lamp across from the foundry entrance so he would see her through the bluish-yellow haze.

∾

Tom approached the massive metal door and thought of it as an escape hatch from the endless hours of confinement in the intense, heat-laden existence.

He grasped the handle and pulled the door along its pulley restraint. Once outside, Tom heard several men exchanging cynical comments about a small figure standing at the end of the walkway.

"Hey, Tom, you got a minder to show you the way home tonight, aye?"

He rushed over, took Mary by the shoulders and pulled her close to him. "Woman, what were you thinking walking these streets alone."

Mary stepped back, removed the letter and handed it to him. "A post came today from your mum."

He scanned the envelope and put it in his pocket.

"Please, won't you open it, Tom?"

"When we get to the flats."

Her eyes widened. "No, now. I want to know what it says."

He took the letter out, opened it and began reading silently to himself.

"You're joking me; what does it say, Tom?"

He handed it to her and raised an eyebrow. "You don't mind now, do you?"

Mary drew in a deep breath.

Dear Tom,

We're relieved that you and Mary are well but feel your decision to leave as you did, risking Mary's safety and that of your baby, was a brazen one that needs our forgiveness and your humility. We're sorry for the loss of your baby and would like you both to come home now. Our families are in agreement. If the cost for your journey is hard to come by, we'll pay for the trip once you've come to your senses.

Love, Mum and Dad.

~

"Tom, they want us to come home. Sure it's not what we thought this would be like here."

"One day you'll go back in fine style, Mary. Until then, you have to trust me."

She glared at him, wrapped the scarf across her chin and whipped it over one shoulder. A storm of feelings brewed as she stomped off.

"What are you doing, Mary?"

She stopped and spun around, pulled off her gloves and held her palms up. "Just look at me hands from stirring Moss's so-called stew of civil servant uniforms. And I'm so tired of living in this cesspool."

Mary lowered her head and then looked up at him with pleading eyes. "I just want to go home, Tom."

She turned and walked ahead of him; her footsteps click-clacked along the cobblestone street.

Chapter 13

Not One More Night

"I've some good news," Angela announced. "The O'Connors just picked up and left early this morning without any notice."

"So that means you two can move your worldly goods upstairs right after the workday tomorrow," Gracey said.

"It's a nicer flat than most of them," Angela noted. "Farther from the sewers and facing south."

"And we'll be neighbors, to boot," Gracey added. She looked away and stepped back. Tom walked over to Mary and gave her a glimmer of a smile.

"We'll take it," she said softly.

Angela nodded. "I'll get a key to you in the morning."

They all jumped to a loud clattering beyond the front door. Donnie stumbled in, belched and glanced around. "Hello, Your Grace."

"Ah! You're off your face again. I see Moss grabbed you before you could hightail it home."

"For your information, me and Moss were at Kilcullens discussing some business about the O'Connor's flat."

"Oh really, and just what were you two geniuses discussing about it?"

Donnie raised his chin in the air. "Well, Moss let it be known, only to me, that Paddy O'Connor's flat might be empty by a fortnight. And I was telling Moss that it might be a fine idea for Tom and Mary to move in next to us. So what do you say about that, Grace?"

"Sure's a waste of time you've been babbling on so. We already know that, and it's not a fortnight at all. For your information, the O'Connors are gone. Me and Angela already started cleaning up the gaff to ready for the Clementses."

Donnie scratched his head and knit his eyebrows. "Who are the Clementses anyway?"

"Why, Tom and Mary, you fool."

Donnie muttered something unintelligible as he staggered down the hall.

$$\sim$$

The next day, Mary was carrying some rubbish to a bin along the back alley. The lid was propped up and overflowing. She looked around and spied another bin at the end of the building. She continued on, and when she opened it, there lay a small blood-stained mattress. Mary dropped the lid, ran back into the building and hurried up the stairs. She felt nauseous as her chest rose and fell with rapid breaths.

Tom, Donnie and Moss appeared through the door.

"Moss said the flat's all ours, and I've got the key," Tom said. "Let's have a look, aye?"

He unlocked the door, and they entered the room. A cradle stood in front of a window, empty of any bedding.

Moss's eyes darted around the room as he shifted his weight. "That's all they left. We thought you might be wanting it some day."

Mary walked over to Moss with a piercing stare and shook her head vehemently. "I'll have nothing to do with that cradle. Tom, I'll be right back. I need a word with Gracey."

≈

Mary's brows dropped, and her lips pursed. "Tell me now, Gracey. You think I'm thick as a ditch to the goings-on around here? You knew about the mattress." Mary's eyes narrowed. "You knew about this, didn't you. I know the baby died in that room, and that's why they left."

"I'm sorry, Mary. I don't know how the wee one passed, poor thing. I heard him coughing fierce the night before. When the O'Connors left, Moss told me to get rid of the mattress and to keep it on the quiet."

Mary bit her lip; her eyes glistened. "We were going to live there, Gracey. Why didn't you tell me?"

"Mary, I just couldn't find it in me to tell you."

Mary backed away. "Aye, I suppose you couldn't then. Well, Tom's waiting on me, so I'll be going now."

"Please, Mary, come in. I'll go wet the tea, and we'll talk."

"Don't be troubling yourself."

Tears gathered behind Mary's lids, and the space around them burned. She left without so much as a backward glance.

Gracey strained a whisper, "I love you, Mary."

~

Tom remained at the window of the flat. Rain pounded on the glass. Mary joined him, and they looked across the dilapidated rooftops, rodent-infested alleys and garbage-strewn streets. Mary told him about the mattress as they viewed an old woman rummage through a garbage bin.

"We're leaving before the sun's up," Tom said.

Mary looked up at him and nodded with a single dip of her chin. "I'm glad I left Ireland with you, and I'm glad we're leaving this kip of a place. Let's pack up and get some sleep downstairs. I won't stay in this room a minute longer."

~

Well before daybreak, Tom rapped twice on Donnie and Gracey's door. Donnie opened it.

"Tom, what are you doing here at this hour?" he whispered. "I haven't had me breakfast or even me tea."

"Come into the hall for a wee minute."

Donnie called out, "Grace, keep the kettle on; I'll be right back."

"Mary and I are leaving the city," Tom said.

"Jaysus, Mary and Joseph, Tom! Where will you go?"

"We're not sure - somewhere far from this city way of life. I don't have time to explain. Mary is waiting. When we get settled, I'll write you where we are. Mary and Gracey will surely mend their fences."

"Tom, we can't go anywhere. I mean, we have jobs and a place to live. Moss and Angela are the only family we have. We can't just get up and leave all this."

Donnie waved his hand around as if he were showing off a place of elegance and charm instead of the dingy, dimly lit hall which had never seen a lick of paint.

"You two go before Moss shows up. I'll say I never heard a word."

Tom and Donnie gripped hands and hugged an awkward hug.

"I appreciate all you've done for us, Donnie. You and Gracey have been good friends. I'll always remember the pair of you. Take good care of her, and take it easy on the gargle."

~

The dense, early morning fog loomed along the alleyway. It was almost tangible, shrouding Manhattan in a thick white veil. Wearing a wool tweed cap and sack coat, Tom pulled their trunk, now tied onto a metal frame with wheels. Mary wore a touch of color on her lips. Her long wool coat, black hose and black laced shoes all spoke of a package that proclaimed she was properly dressed. Tom slowed his pace, and Mary fell in step beside him. She held her head high, and the corners of his mouth lifted as they continued for Chatham Square and ultimately Grand Central Station.

Chapter 14

May It Be

Tom felt uneasy when they arrived at Grand Central, not so much because he was an Irishman in America, for he was certain that on this large train platform walked dozens of Irish, though most were from the Republic. He observed men with briefcases or lunch boxes who seemed to know exactly where they were going, which train to catch and from which platform. Tom quickly realized he needed to be valiant — plain and simple.

Tom and Mary wove through a crowd of various languages and dialects. He held her hand as they approached the Grand Lobby. They gazed up at a mural of tiny stars across the cathedral-like ceiling. Tom looked over at a sign which read *All Trains To Buffalo*.

"When might your next train be leaving for Buffalo?" he asked.

The man behind the counter lolled his head to one side. "The next train out leaves in fifteen minutes with two stops. Looks like you just made it."

"I'll take two tickets, please."

The man tapped the counter, and Tom slid his money under the window.

"If you'll be wanting a meal, it'll cost you more than what I see here."

Mary tugged on Tom's coat and shook her head.

"That won't be needed," Tom said.

They left the station and waited by the tracks with other passengers steadily filling the gaps behind them. For Tom, a sense of confidence had returned, the kind he had the morning he joined the sun at daybreak to find Mary. It was good to be back there again.

An indecipherable announcement flickered over the loud-speaker. The crowd began to push their way along the platform further narrowing the already limited space. Tom tightened his grip on Mary's hand.

The stationmaster called out, "All aboard the 6:15 for Albany, Rochester and Buffalo."

They found themselves in the last car looking through a clouded window smeared with the telltale grime they were leaving behind. Mary curled her arm through Tom's, and they laid their heads back as the train crawled out of the station heading north and west.

The conductor worked his way along the aisle. "Tickets, tickets, have your tickets ready."

Tom reached into his pocket and handed the man their tickets.

"What can you tell us about Buffalo, sir?" Mary asked.

"Mostly factory work and lots of snow. I don't know much, Madam. I just run back and forth with the trains. I live here in the City."

"I see, and do you fancy your job on the trains?"

He walked away mumbling, "It's what I do Madam, that's all."

Mary set her satchel on her lap, opened it and pulled out a crumpled brown paper bag.

"What's this?" Tom asked.

"Soda bread and jam. They were on the steps when I went up to the loo this morning."

"Gracey?"

"I suppose."

"We're going to miss those two, ya know," Tom said.

"I suppose."

The train clattered on, and they ate in silence pondering their time with Donnie and Gracey. Tom cradled Mary in the crook of his arm. He lowered his shoulders, she nestled against his chest and slept. Tom peered at the sun's rays rise up the oaks waking the valleys dotted with cattle and stilled horses. It cascaded across low sweeping hills pushing its light through the dusty windows of the train. It seemed to be announcing a day to remember as it melted the blankets of fog which stubbornly lingered in the crevices of this picturesque land. The train was quiet now, almost gliding. A rooster crowed in the distance. Tom dozed off.

Tom and Mary woke as the train rumbled into an Albany depot where they were joined by a handful of passengers.

"How much longer do you think we've got to go?" Mary asked.

Tom gave her an affectionate squeeze. "As long as it takes. Let's get some more sleep. It'll surely shorten the trip."

When they left Rochester, they passed by several horse farms with white fencing which stretched far beyond the green meadows. Colonies of lily pads displayed their wide leaves floating on the surface of a pond framed with cattails and duckweed. This countryside brought Tom a sense of contentment much like the land back home always did. A subtle smile crossed his lips.

Chapter 15

Breakdown

Soon, a loud clamoring arose from the front of the train. It snaked onto an alternate track and came to a long, screeching stop before a stationary caboose.

"Ladies and gentlemen, it seems we have a steam pump needing our attention," the engineer announced. "We'll be delayed in order to repair it. Feel free to roam but best be back in three hours."

"Let's get something to eat," Mary said as they stepped down from the train.

A horse driven hay wagon pulled up next to them. The driver lightly snapped the reins against a muscular draft horse who plodded past them and stopped alongside the first class passenger car. The wagon had been cleaned out and lined with sturdy benches. Mary eyed the affluent women file off the train wearing impressive clothes and hats like those on the *Cedric,* she thought. Tom read the words along the side of the wagon: Avonvale, finest Stallions and Mares.

The driver flipped a toothpick in his mouth. "You're in Avon, folks. Anybody want a ride to the county fair? It's about a mile and a half down by the river. I'm Murdock, the foreman at Avonvale, and we're showing some fine horses with bloodlines second to none. Well worth your inspection, I might add. You missed the parade of stallions, but the horse races and dressage competitions are a sight to behold."

Murdock awkwardly climbed down from the wagon and pulled out a large wood crate from beneath his bench seat. With a grunt, he jacked it up on one shoulder. Bottles clinked as he limped over to the wood platform. He slid the crate across to the station's entrance. A man appeared at the door and stopped it with his foot.

"There you go, you scalawag," Murdock said.

He hobbled back, flashed a charming smile at an attractive young woman and eagerly helped her onto the back of the wagon. He turned to Mary and held out his hand. "The more the merrier," he said with a persuasive charm.

Tom quickly retrieved her hand. "Don't be troubling yourself."

"Suit yourselves, but you won't find anything open in town if you're looking for something to eat. They're all at the fair."

Murdock climbed up, flipped the toothpick and snapped the reigns. Tom and Mary looked on as the rattling wagon and chattering passengers pulled away.

"I saw him slip the engineer a wad of cash, and that crate is surely payment to the station attendant," Tom said. "This three-hour delay is indeed not by chance. There's likely some buyers for Avonvale's horses in that lot we traveled with. Let's wait 'til they're out of sight, then we'll just walk down — the smart arse."

"So stretch our legs we will," Mary announced.

~

"Oh, Tom. Isn't this grand?"

Mary delighted in the sights and sounds of people trying their luck dinging bells and spinning wheels to win plush stuffed animals, trinkets and treasures. The aromas of cotton candy, roasted peanuts, buttered steamed potatoes and fresh corn-on-the-cob barely outweighed the odors of manure from all kinds of farm animals competing for the winner's circle.

Mary inhaled a deep breath through her nose. The wind's direction favored the barn yards with echoes of happier times. "Almost reminds you of home, don't you think, Tom?"

"Aye, it surely does," he said with a wistful smile.

People walked through muddy ruts dredged by many feet along the midway. The music of fiddlers and bark of carnival workers, enticing young and old into their lairs, sent their senses reeling. Women of self importance swished about in their dresses of taffeta with crinoline petticoats. They pranced above the mud on wood planks which had been laid over the grounds for only those of wealth and status. Violet and deep purple lavenders seemed to be the favored colors, Mary thought. Black, hard felt bowler hats sat snugly on nearly every man's head.

"Wouldn't you be fitting wearing one of those, Tom? And while you're at it, you could buy me one of those fancy ladies' hats."

"At least let me earn me first dollar here before you go making Mr. Sears & Mr. Roebuck even richer."

Tom's eyes shined at the sound of her lilting laughter as they strolled along the midway eating their first hot dogs ladened with mustard and pickle relish.

∽

A man stood in the center of the main riding ring calling out the names of each horse as their trainers led them around in a controlled, orderly fashion.

Manes and tails were braided; their coats gleamed. Hooves were painted and polished to a sheen. Tom marveled at the hunters and jumpers as they worked hard against the soft rain-soaked surface.

One woman competing in a jumping event tussled with her horse as he continually reared up when approaching the first jump. She was compelled to dismount and withdraw from the competition after several patient and gritty unsuccessful attempts to settle him down.

Tom stepped out and steadily walked over to the wide-eyed, skittish animal. With a soft movement, he stroked the stallion's withers. His voice lay smooth on the air as he took hold of the bridle. Tom felt the horse's hot breath sweep over his face. The horse pawed at the ground, and Tom saw an anxiousness in his eyes that he, himself, had been feeling for several months. To his surprise, a calm connection, an understanding of some kind, graciously evolved between Tom and this horse.

"Take him back around and give him another chance, won't you now."

The rider looked to the judges' table. They nodded. Tom gave her a leg up, and her horse brought home second place on that eventful day when Tom felt he was drawn to a life with horses.

Murdock stood next to Mary shaking his head. A distinguished looking silver-haired man with a mustache of the same walked up and reached for Tom's hand.

"So you have a way with horses. I've never seen anything quite like that before. I'm C. L. Whiting, the owner of Avonvale."

He shook Tom's hand and gave him a steady look. "What is your name, Son?"

"Tom Clements, and this is me wife, Mary."

A man called out. "If you're looking for work, I'm needing a man at Fairwind Stables."

"Hire him, Murdock."

"But, Boss, we brought on someone just last week. We really don't need another hand."

C. L. looked him square in the eyes. "Hire him, I said."

Tom's mouth turned up at the corners.

"Sound good to you, young man?"

"Yes, sir. It surely does."

"When can he start?" Mary asked.

"Right away. I've got some other business to tend to while Murdock gets you settled in."

"Meet me at the wagon in about an hour," Murdock said. "I'll round up the others, and we'll head back to the train for your gear before delivering your wife at Avonvale. I hope you're no stranger to back-breaking work, Irish. Packing up from the fair will take us well past sunset."

Murdock reached into his shirt pocket and pulled out another toothpick. "Good thing you didn't take work at one of those sweat shops off the boat. Looks like this work's going to suit you, Irish."

Murdock flipped the toothpick.

Chapter 16

Coming Home

Murdock clicked his tongue and tapped the reins.

"First of all, always refer to C. L.'s wife as Madame. She's not French but claims it's in her blood. She's what you call eccentric or just plain nuts, if you ask me. She insisted that C. L. import a French maid direct from Paris. Turns out Celeste didn't speak a word of English."

"Does Madame speak French?" Mary asked.

"Nope," Murdock chortled.

"That drove Madame even more nuts than she already is, so she told C. L. to send her back after only a few months. Then, he had me take the little filly to Rochester and leave her with a train ticket to New York and passage back to France."

They stopped before a private drive. An arched sign flanked two red brick columns. Mary craned her neck and read the bold lettering above: "AVONVALE"

She nudged Tom and her mouth quirked to the side. "This must be the place."

Murdock twisted around.

"This brings us to the boss. Good thing he's loaded, and I mean loaded. C. L. Whiting is the most successful horse breeder around. He knows the history of every horse in the valley including who sired who. I've been with him for over seventeen years, and all you really need to know is that he's a fair man to work for who doesn't tolerate any form of incompetence when it comes to his horses. Always remember that, Irish. You're going to either make it or break it here, and my gut says you'll do just fine."

Tom stared thoughtfully ahead as they continued along the serpentine driveway. His gaze riveted on the lush countryside and pinkish hue of the late afternoon sun in contrast to the bleak urban landscape of the city life they had left behind.

Swaying conifers and graceful willows thrust about by insistent breezes. Mary closed her eyes and breathed in the bouquet of Honeysuckle and Jasmine still in bloom.

When she opened them, a magnificent red brick mansion stood before them. Mary peered up at a railed roof walk encircling a small square tower, windows encompassing the structure. Immaculate white stables with black trim appeared beyond several rows of white fences that separated numerous paddocks, pastures and the entire property from the rest of the world. Several spirited horses enjoyed the crisp air, strutting their stuff as if they knew an audience was present.

The wagon horse quickened his pace along the drive and onto a worn tractor path leading to a small bungalow.

Mary leaned in. "Look, Tom, Avonvale has a Green Road of its own."

"Well, this is it. Pretty basic. Let's get your trunk in and be off," Murdock said.

Mary glanced around the room and walked over to a window, her eyes following a garden spider spinning its web.

She ran her fingers along a filmy windowpane. "It looks like I have me work cut out, and I see I won't be alone for long." A curious smile crossed her lips.

A woman with bright orange hair trudged up the path carrying a broom in one hand and her shoes in the other.

"That's Madame Whiting," Murdock said to Mary as he boarded the wagon. "Some days she's the lady of the manor and other days, well, you're about to see for yourself. She's all yours, darlin'."

Tom leaned over, kissed Mary's cheek and climbed up. "I see she's about your height. Guess that puts you on equal ground, aye?"

Mary smiled up at him. "You're a corker, you are, Tom Clements."

The wagon passed by the peculiar appearing Madame. Murdock bowed his head and tipped his cap.

Madame shot a wild look at him.

"Damn Murdock, have you gained weight?" Then she turned to Mary raising her chin. "What are you gawking at? Haven't you ever seen a dye job before?"

Madame held the broom out to Mary. "You will be needing this is my guess. The place is most likely a pigsty. The hired hands stayed here before the bunkhouse was built, and it has been empty ever since."

She harrumphed. "So I see Murdock brought on another hand. Your husband, I gather. It's a good thing since Murdock's worth is limited after a half-breed gave him a swift kick a while back. Before that, he actually took a fine seat in the riding ring, but don't tell *him* I said that. I suppose my husband keeps him on to pick up the slack with a few minute details when he is off doing who knows what."

She turned and walked away muttering something about her rose garden, but as Mary scanned the area, she saw no signs of one.

"Madame, me name is Mary."

Madame stopped dead in her tracks, reeled around and stood with arms akimbo. "What did you call me?"

"You're Madame Whiting, to be sure?"

"How did you know that? Oh, never mind. How are you at ironing and formal table setting and following orders, for that matter?"

"Excuse me, Madame, but I can handle any work you throw me way, and it'll always be spot on."

Madame stood her tallest with regal authority. "We will see about that. You will prepare our breakfasts, and I will leave a list of further instructions. Familiarize yourself with the kitchen beforehand. It is organized to my specifications, and it will stay that way. Any questions?"

"No, Madame."

"Oh shoot," Madame said snapping her fingers. "I forgot one thing. I don't know where you're from, but around here we catch the fish, rip out its guts and slap it in the pan, tout suite."

Madame picked up her shoes and walked back to the house.

Mary had no doubt that she could handle the work. She shivered at the grandeur of their new home. She loved being at Avonvale.

Chapter 17

Brand New Day

The following morning, C. L. sat at the dining room table study-ing a racing form and savoring two fried eggs, pork sausages and warm buttered biscuits. He peered over the top of his glasses and watched Mary pour strong breakfast coffee ladened with heavy sweet cream. She returned the silver pot to the credenza and stood next to it. Her eyes followed a myriad of colors reflecting from the vast crystal chandelier hanging in the adjoining room. A library table with heavy scroll legs and turned feet supported a massive, ornate vase brimming with long-stemmed red roses.

"Thank you, Mary," C. L. muttered and turned the page. "The roses are from the local farmers market. They're replaced weekly, whether they need to be or not."

"They're lovely," Mary said as Madame waltzed into the room, sat at the far end of the table and placed her hands in her lap. Mary noticed her studying the intricate table setting which Mary had arranged precisely to Madame's instructions. She popped into the kitchen then promptly returned with two poached eggs, crisp bacon and a croissant all creatively arranged on elegant china. She set the plate in front of Madame with care, returned to the credenza and removed a small porcelain teapot.

"Would Madame like me to pour her a cup of lemon verbena?"

"Yes, Mary, I would please."

When Mary started to insert a wooden dipper into the honey pot, Madame took her hand. "There's a method to this so as not to drizzle any honey along the way. Allow me."

Madame took the dipper, and Mary watched her intently.

"Twirl the wand into that sweet, sticky liquid. Keep twisting it as you lift the tip out and over to the cup. Then simply turn the dipper downward." They peered into the teacup and watched the honey flow freely.

Madame looked up at Mary with a pleasing smile. "Voila."

A smile tugged at the corners of Mary's lips as she unfolded a white linen napkin and laid it across Madame's lap.

C. L spoke without looking up from his paper. "And she speaks English, to boot."

"That will be all, Mary." Madame glared at C. L. then indulged herself with pleasure.

Mary paused and observed the two of them: silent, disconnected, unmoving. She thought of the evening ahead when she and Tom would be holding each other in their bungalow.

∾

Madame folded her arms across her chest and scowled at Mary.

"What in Sam Hill do you think you are doing with that spade? Haven't you enough to do inside?"

"I'm tidying up your rose garden, Madame. I've collected a boatload of lily of the valley from the woods to make a lovely blanket for them. And what do you think of having some white and cream roses climbing up your gazebo?"

"Gazebo? What gazebo? I don't have a gazebo," she said crisply.

"They're for the one Tom's building you. In the spring, your garden will be a place of rare beauty," Mary said.

Madame stood quietly, and then she tilted her head to one side. A pleasing smile crossed her lips.

"Yes, it will be splendid with our white and cream roses, not so dramatic as the red ones, don't you think, Mary?"

"Aye, I think you're onto something there, Madame."

A shadow fell across Madame's brow. "But will I be able to view the wisteria tree when I'm seated inside?"

"Of course you will. Tom will see to that."

They looked at each other for a long moment then surveyed the area of dense brambles and woody weeds that would become their rose garden.

"Well, don't just stand there, let's get to work." Madame began pulling weeds.

Chapter 18

Awakening

The following spring, little sprays of delicate bell-like flowers spread gracefully throughout the area offering their distinct sweet perfume. Strands of white and cream rosebuds began taking on their wild side as they interlaced their way up the latticed walls. Giant purple flowers exploded throughout the wisteria tree offering their own creamy vanilla scent which heralded the entranceway to Madame's sanctuary.

Madame sat on a white wrought iron bench beneath the peaked hardwood roof. She removed her silk hose and shoes and inhaled deeply, filling her lungs with the infused fragrances that made her think of her childhood, light and carefree.

Mary sat back on her calves pulling weeds and tossing them into a bushel basket.

"You know, Celeste spoke only French, and I wasn't informed prior to her arrival," Madame said. She squirmed. "C. L. didn't seem to mind though. And then why would he?

The louse didn't need to communicate with her. And with that innocent French demure she overstated, flitting about the house displaying a set of boobies that could give a man my husband's age a heart attack; well, I saw right through her. I was surprised C. L. didn't even flinch with my decision to dismiss her. I'm glad he at least had the sense this time to hire a married woman — a woman like you, Mary."

Mary got up, walked over to Madame and sat next to her.

Madame hung her head. "But, Mary, I still feel her presence around every corner I turn. It's eerie, damn eerie. It's as though I may not have had the last word."

"She's gone now, and I'm here." Feeling Madame's despair, she turned to her friend, took her trembling hands and held them between her own.

Madame faced Mary. A smirk crossed her lips. "Come to the creek with me. I have something to show you."

~

They walked along a bank to a shallow cove where the water had become stagnant. Madame squatted close to the water's edge. Her upper body seemed to fall across her bent-up knees, like an old rag doll. She began flipping over small, flat rocks until she uncovered a leech. "There you are, Mademoiselle."

Mary crouched close to her.

Madame stuck her toes in the mud and watched the leech inch its way in her direction.

"Let's go back so you can take a wee nap, Madame."

"They latch on and will suck the blood out of its prey until they're satisfied," Madame said completely deadpan. She let her shoulders droop and her head sag. "Know any people like the leech, Mary?"

Mary helped her up, and they walked arm in arm toward the house. Madame stopped before the gazebo.

"Wait here." She walked over, gathered her hose and shoes and handed them to Mary.

~

One afternoon, Madame overheard C. L. during a telephone conversation with his attorney. She braced herself along the wall in the adjoining room.

"I want you to have her committed to the sanatorium. You need to find her mentally unstable which I'm sure won't be a problem. I'll have Murdock back that up in court. Oh, and Victor, I will be awarded Avonvale, of course."

Madame white-knuckled the console table next to her and stifled an overwhelming urge to lash out. Glancing down, she observed a photo of them from so many years before. She noticed that even then their faces looked stale. She had all the money, and he had all the drive to be a success leaving little of his time for their marriage. It hadn't been long for both of them to feel no more than two people who shared the same dead space, she thought.

Madame retreated to her boudoir and sat at her vanity beside a soft ray of light peeking through the window. In the mirror's reflection, she eyed the grand canopy bed with gold shears draping like a delicate circus tent. This bed had not known the gaiety or passions of love and laughter for over four decades.

She picked up the sterling silver hairbrush which once belonged to his mother and lightly caressed the cameo centered on its back. This gift made her feel so special. Turning the brush over, she ran her aching, knotty fingers across the soft bristles that stroked her once-shiny shoulder-length hair. They now leaned over to one side like a fragile willow in a windy storm.

Protruding veins traveled in sad, twisting formations along her hands as if fighting for life. Raising her eyes to the oval mirror, she studied her now dull, brittle hair. She examined the contours of her face with its endless fine lines, its symmetry revealing her equally transparent, pallid complexion. How pathetic, she thought. The attempts with sexy French nightgowns were long gone and with them the love she had for a man whose eyes once lit up whenever she entered a room.

Madame set the brush back on her vanity. No longer smooth, warm and dainty, she helplessly observed her trembling hand hover over it, now keeping company with red and brown spots, too many to count. The only thing steady was a stream of silent tears that flowed down her cheeks and into the small white lace doily which draped the table top. The powder from her nose left a creamy, wet stain.

A flash of anger swept away her sadness, and she focused her thoughts on C. L. Madame's adrenaline surged, and with one fell swoop, her arms hurled every item on the table into the air.

Her brushes, powders and perfumes crashed to the floor.

Then, she hypnotically rose and walked to the window where a small table stood. She picked up the gold jeweled music box he had given her. She opened it, and the trembling resumed increasing its magnitude. Madame wrestled with this malady preventing her to hold the box still and listen to its lovely song. She shut her eyes to skirt out the pain, and then she smashed the box on the table. It shattered and joined the rest.

Shrugging, Madame stood facing the mirror. Complacent and still, she rolled magenta lipstick over her lips, pushed them out just a little and laughed to herself. Then, she reached for a tissue, dabbed the corners of her eyes and picked up the phone.

Chapter 19

Sometimes When It Rains

"*Operator, please connect* me with Mr. Dupont's office. It's an urgent matter."

"Right away, Madame." A short silence ensued.

"Thank you for calling the law office of Pierre DuPont. How may I help you?"

"This is Madame Whiting. I would like to speak with Pierre, please."

"Good afternoon, Madame. If you will kindly hold, I'll see if he is available."

A man's voice came across the wire in seconds. "Madame, so good to hear from you. And how is everything at Avonvale this fine day?"

"Well, getting down to it, Pierre, I overheard my husband talking with his attorney, and I decided to call you at once. This is not only to protect myself but to develop a counterstrategy."

"Madame, are you alright? What is going on?"

"He's a wicked man, wicked," she said. "He's planning to have me committed and have Avonvale all to himself. Surely there are laws to protect a woman such as myself. If anyone should have the whole of Avonvale, why, it should be me, of course. My money was what started this place. The audacity of him to label me as a crazy woman. It's unfathomable that I should be displaced at his whim."

"I'm here for you, Madame. When you plan your next trip to the city, I will meet you at my office and get to the bottom of this. First of all, one must have due cause to move forward with this type of proceeding."

"I will be there promptly at ten tomorrow morning."

"Very well, Madame. I'll be expecting you."

"Thank you, Pierre. Goodbye."

Madame walked over to her vanity, looked in the mirror, and for a few precious moments she saw a woman with the beauty and dignity she had always known as Catherine.

～

Madame sat under her gazebo, her dull, gray eyes without expression as she watched Mary tidy up their rose beds. A mosquito whined in her ear. Madame rocked back and forth, her fingers clasped around the edge of the bench, her arms rigid. Mary felt her uneasiness, joined Madame on the bench and waved off the mosquito.

"Two can play at this game," Madame said. "Did he expect I'd steal off like a mouse?" She stretched her neck upward, her body distorted like a question mark. "I shelved my own dreams in order to follow his."

She stomped on a large beetle attempting to make its escape. She smirked. "Did you know the Mona Lisa has no eyebrows? I believe most people don't. Isn't that just remarkable, Mary?"

"No, I didn't know that, Madame."

Madame flipped her head back and laughed out loud. "The bastard has gone off with the French bitch, I'm getting older than water, and now I'm all alone."

She took quick, deep breaths and scanned the ground as if she was searching for a sense of collectiveness.

"What do you mean, Madame?"

"I had C. L. followed."

Madame raised her head and scrambled to her feet. She walked to the garden and snapped off a rose.

"He and that French whore were cozied up in a hotel lobby nuzzling each other like two dogs in heat. Imagine that," she scoffed. "I'll show that snake."

"But, Madame, I thought he sent her back to France."

"Apparently not." Madame studied the flower and wrapped her hand around its thorny stem.

"I'd like to pinch her nose between my fingers and squeeze hard." Her voice was implacable.

"Madame, what are you doing?"

Mary lunged forward and grabbed Madame's wrist. She methodically pried Madame's fingers from the piercing thorns and guided her back to the gazebo. Mary pulled a hankie from under the strap of her brassiere and wrapped it around the injured hand. Madame's face crumpled, and when the words wouldn't come, the tears did.

"Of all the cheek. And after all you've done for him," Mary said.

Madame blew her nose on the corner of her skirt. "Sometimes I feel I'm unraveling, but madness isn't madness until someone calls it that. Isn't that right, Mary?"

Mary put her arm around Madame. "You'll never be alone as long as I'm alive."

Clouds had been massing and darkening. The sky began spitting a light rain accompanied by a low, distant rumble.

"I knew he was a cheat," she sniffled, "but my heart just played along. Most men are born to betray, you know."

Mary held out her arm. Madame took ahold of it, and they strolled back toward the house.

In moments they were soaked.

Chapter 20

Letting Go

C. L. removed his glasses and polished them vehemently while pacing his attorney's office. The moment his attorney put the phone down, C. L. sat across from him, his leg bouncing up and down in a nervous tic.

"Damn it, Victor! What the hell am I going to do now? The whole facade is over, and I have to get the hell out of here."

"Look, C. L., you are seventy-two, and you've got plenty of cash, think about it. You can afford any lifestyle with your little filly. To avoid a scandal and to be with her, grab as much cash as you can and give your half of the estate to your wife or someone like Murdock or that Irish boy you're so fond of."

C. L. twisted the wedding ring on his finger. "You must be kidding."

Victor leaned back in his chair, his fingers clasped over his vest. "We've been friends a long time Charles, and if you really want my advice, I say gift it and avoid all the mess."

C. L. walked to the window and looked at his reflection. He loosened his tie, and his lips held a faint smile. "You're right, my friend. This couldn't be more perfect. Celeste is the best thing that has happened to me in a long time."

C. L. sat down and slapped his thighs. "I would do anything to be with her. Murdock's getting up there and won't be sticking around with this work for long. I'm sure he wouldn't object to a generous severance pay to accompany his retirement. Besides, we both know Murdock and Madame would only kill each other." He shook his head and chuckled.

"Victor, I'm going to assign my half of Avonvale to Tom Clements. He'll bring Avonvale to its full potential, which is the least I can do for all his efforts and loyalty over the years. And besides, I have all the money I would ever need. Write it up, and I'll sign. Tom Clements won't let Avonvale down; I'm sure of that."

A veil of peace swept over his face, an air of restful confidence for his decision.

Victor leaned back in his chair, stoic and unmoved. "Consider it done."

～

C. L. strolled around his estate soaking in all the sights, sounds and smells of a place he created and nurtured for well over half of his life. A stormy sky loomed overhead as his prize horses displayed their edgy paces in a nearby pasture. As he turned to leave, the wind seemed to push him forward. The cypress bowed down as he continued back to where Murdock waited at the open car door.

"Let's get the hell out of here before the brigade gets back from the city," C. L. said as he climbed in.

His instinct to look back was outweighed by his thoughts of the young French woman who was waiting for him. Her seductive eyes and soft pink lips lingered in his mind.

Murdock studied C. L.'s eager face in the rearview mirror. "What's the hurry, Boss?"

"I'll explain once we're out of the driveway. For now, don't spare the horses."

A train whistled in the distance as they drove away.

"Murdock, there's going to be a few changes around here. I have some good news and some bad news for you. What do you want to hear first?"

"I suppose the bad news."

"Murdock, as long as I've known you, that has been your problem. You always look for the bad news, and you're never found wanting."

Murdock looked into the mirror's reflective image of a man he thought he'd come to know so well. "What's this all about, Boss?"

"Murdock, you are an uncomplicated man and extremely knowledgeable when it comes to horses. You have been my devoted friend and confidant. I couldn't have brought Avonvale to where it is without you; we both know this. Your loyalty has made me a legend, so to speak. From the beginning you knew I loved this way of life and all Madame brought to the table."

C. L. Looked up at his driver in the mirror.

"Remember when we called her Catherine? She was a beauty back then and had the money to bring my dreams for Avonvale to life." Maple and oak trees reflected in his eyes as he placidly stared out the window.

"Don't get me wrong, I did love her when she was Catherine and all there in the head. Sorry if that sounds heartless, but I didn't sign up for the unhinged Madame. What I'm trying to say is that by joining her fortune to begin with and your horse breeding sense, I became highly respected contrary to the myth behind my success. We fooled everyone, even my wife."

C. L. sat forward and again eyed Murdock in the mirror. "I'm leaving town. I'm taking Celeste to her hometown south of Paris, and I'm not coming back. I've had her stashed in Rochester, and now Madame has got the goods on me. It seems her attorney, who shares a liking for the same hotel bar and restaurant as I do, got wind that I've been spending time there with Celeste."

"What? You and Celeste? What are you talking about? I thought she was long gone."

"You bought that hook, line and sinker, didn't you? Come on man, don't tell me you didn't really know. Anyway, I love her loads, and she says she loves me some. That's good enough for me. If I stick around, the shenanigans involved will be unbearable. Madame will do all she can to crucify me." C. L. winced and shook his head. "So it's easier to give my half of Avonvale away. And to be honest, I had considered you. But let's face it, besides the fact that you really wouldn't want to tackle this magnitude of responsibility now, you'd never be able to make peace with *The Madame* near good enough to keep the place from getting cut in two."

"You mean you're just walking away from Avonvale?"

"You're quite perceptive, my good man." A wry smile crossed C. L.'s lips. "And believe it or not, I decided to give my half to that nice young Irish couple. The kid has a head on his shoulders and will sweat bullets to keep the business where I've taken it and then some. Tom Clements will also get along with the former Mrs. Whiting. So I'm grabbing some loot and heading to France. Take a right here; I'm going to the Landmark Hotel."

"But, Boss, what about the good news?"

C. L. leaned forward and slapped him on his shoulder. "Don't pass out from the excitement, Murdock, but there's a bag in the trunk for you. You'll never want for anything as long as you live, my friend."

C. L. walked through the revolving front door of Rochester's finest hotel. In the distance, he could make out her silhouette, sleek and fluid like her smile at early dawn when light from the sun begins to appear. The scent of jasmine and caramel spoke only of Celeste.

Chapter 21

Catherine

Soon after C. L. left, Tom, Mary and Victor sat around a small table at the bungalow.

"Thank you for agreeing to meet here," Victor said. "It was Madame's idea." He shrugged his shoulders and slid an envelope across the table.

"What's this?" Tom asked.

"C.L. asked me to give this to you. I thought you'd want to know about its contents before Madame arrives. She will be informed shortly along with her attorney by her side, of course."

"Might you read it aloud, if you don't mind?" Tom slid the envelope back and sat upright, his hands curled over the armrests.

"Very well," Victor said. He opened it and looked over at Tom and Mary, their eyes wide with anticipation.

Mr. Clements:

First of all, I'm leaving Avonvale for reasons I'm sure you'll learn about very soon, if not prior to receiving this letter. I have also spoken with Murdock, and he has decided that this would be a good time for him to retire.

Getting down to it, I'm gifting my half of Avonvale to you. I know how much you've come to love it here, and I'm confident that you will bring even greater success to Avonvale. It's the least I can do for all your dedication to the work and your devotion to me over the years. Congratulations, Tom.

All the best,
C. L. Whiting

Tom leaned forward and blinked a few times. "You must be jokin'. He's giving me half of Avonvale?"

"How can this be?" Mary said.

Victor shook his head. "Only in America, my dear, only in America."

"Well, surely this wouldn't happen in Ireland," Tom quipped.

Madame appeared beyond the screen door and began picking off cottonwood seeds which were lodged in its mesh. She shaded her eyes with both hands and squinted hard against the screen.

"Victor, you horse's petute; I thought that was your car. What good news has the grim reaper for me today?"

"Hold on, Madame. Your attorney is on his way, and I'd rather you get the facts from him."

No sooner did Victor get his words out, and Pierre arrived kicking up a tunnel of dust behind him.

"Looks like I won't have to wait long," Madame said.

Pierre gave Madame the French greeting of a peck on both cheeks, opened the door and she sashayed into the room with guarded pride. He escorted her to the table and pulled out a chair. Madame swept the fluted skirt of her cotton frock neatly under her, sat down, folded her hands and placed them in her lap.

"What is this all about, Pierre? You know I won't co-own Avonvale with that reptile and it must remain intact."

"Let me assure you that your partner in the ownership of Avonvale is no longer your husband," Victor said. "This was something he took care of before he left town. It was then my duty to inform Mr. DuPont of C. L.'s part in all this."

Tom reached for Mary's hand under the table.

"I would appreciate it if you would not refer to that no good imbecile as my husband, and I was under the impression that my attorney had been appointed to give me the low down."

She turned to Pierre.

"I will say this could turn out to be a rather fortuitous gathering," Pierre said.

Madame gestured with her chin. "And what do these two have to do with this so-called fortuitous gathering?"

"Well, before C. L. left town, he made arrangements to deed his stake in Avonvale to Tom Clements."

Madame fell back against her chair and jutted her face out with a walleye expression. "You mean our hired hand here?"

Mary squeezed Tom's hand.

"Yes, that's what I said, and if you will let me explain, I think you will conclude he is the best choice. Madame, as you know, I have always looked out for your best interests. For starters, C. L. couldn't sell the property without your signature. So an outright sale was out of the question. Then the conundrum was to whom could he deed his co-ownership to. His first option would have been Murdock, but that would enrage you potentially, and he did not want him to have to deal with the inevitable repercussions."

Madame felt something plummet inside her. "The scumbag called that right. Murdock can be about as ignorant as a stone."

Madame looked squarely at Mary. "Am I going mad?"

Pierre placed his hand on her shoulder. "Please Madame, if you will let me continue. Mr. Clements is young, trustworthy and his future is ahead of him. And I also have something else you may want to seriously think about."

She rolled her eyes. "Oh, what now?"

"You might also entertain selling your half of Avonvale to Mr. Clements with the provision he agree that you remain here until your demise."

Madame inspected her fingernails as the others waited. She smoothed the front of her skirt and placed her hands back on her lap.

"You have my attention, Pierre."

"Also, in exchange for that, you will lower the asking price. How much do you have, Mr. Clements?"

"Three thousand eight hundred dollars plus half the stake in Warrior, the fifteen hander."

"How did you get half in the fifteen hander, Son?"

"Mr. Whiting gave it to me for sitting up with Warrior's foaling mare when he was at the last Canawaugus auction."

"True enough," Victor said. "What Mr. Clements says is correct."

"Oh, shut up, Victor. What are you doing here anyway?"

Madame leaned against the backrest and slowly nodded. Then, she reached in her skirt pocket, took out some cottonwood seeds and set them on the table. Everyone was silent while they watched her stack the tiny white clouds, one by one, into a pile. When she finished, Madame turned toward Tom and Mary and pounded the table with her fist as if it were a gavel.

"Sold! I can't think of anything more exhilarating. I don't even need to think twice about it. As long as I'm treated with the respect due my position as the Lady of the Manor until I croak and they continue to treat me as such, I will agree to the whole kit and caboodle."

Madame cocked her head and winked at Mary. "Truth be known, I have become rather fond of them myself."

A serene smile spread across Mary's face.

"You are a lucky young man, Mr. Clements, the recipient of much generosity," Victor said.

Madame folded her arms over her chest, "So what's the protocol now?"

"Mr. DuPont and I will meet you at my office on Monday and finalize the documents. I believe this arrangement will suit you quite well."

Madame raised her chin. Her voice was controlled and complacent. "Oh, and Victor, as long as you are here, the next time you speak with that insect, tell him if he ever sets foot on Avonvale property, I'll nail his kneecaps to the floor."

Mary gave Tom the side-eye.

Madame slapped her hands flat on the table and rose from her seat. "Meeting adjourned."

They all stood and waited for her to lead the entourage.

"Well, let's get to it, tout suite! We have an estate to run. Mary, I need you in the house. Tom, I need you to do whatever you do in the stables. Pierre, would you be so kind as to escort me out of here."

A smile teased the corner of her mouth. "By the way, you two will need to start talking more like Americans now that you are owners of this magnificent estate and business."

Tom looked at Mary and raised a brow.

"And no need to wait for the legalities to take place. You may just as well move into the big house with me."

Pierre offered his arm, and as they walked away, Madame called over her shoulder, "You will always be Irish you know."

"I'll check that the horses are set for the night," Tom said.

Mary joined Madame along The Green Road.

Chapter 22

Lemon Verbena

Mary sat before a rose tinted oval mirror embedded into an elegant cherry dressing table. The vanity chair was adorned with open scrolls and an upholstered round red velvet seat. It's soft, smooth texture felt warm and luxurious under her. Mary removed the pins from her thick chestnut hair and tossed it about. "I still can't believe all this," she said. "Tom, I'm feeling strangely American tonight. Why is that?"

He lay on the bed, his fingers intertwined on his chest.

"I'm still a wee stunned meself, and you can now refer to me as Your Lordship."

"Oh, is that so?" she said.

Mary stood looking at her image in the mirror. She wore a Blue Chantilly lace and silk-chiffon negligee.

His eyes traveled over her shapely body.

"This negligee came all the way from Paris," she said.

Tom sat on the edge of the bed. His handsome face broke into a slow smile. "Come over here."

Mary looked at his reflection, and her bright eyes locked on his. She turned and walked to him. Tom reached his arms around her and cupped her bottom. He pulled her toward him and looked up at her.

"You're so beautiful."

Mary wanted him more than ever, and she shivered with delight as she straddled him. Her eyes were warm and liquid, full of promise, and her breath quickened as he ran his fingers over the smooth neckline of her bodice. She tipped her head back. Tom strung kisses along her neck, slowly slid the delicate straps over her shoulders and down her arms. He caressed her aroused breasts. She pulled him closer, and he gently kissed one, then the other. Mary felt the heat of her womanly wetness and a hunger in the melting, unexpressed longing as they made love.

∾

Tom got up no earlier and went to bed no later. He managed the business intuitively as did Mary in the house. She went about her duties in the same manner but now paid attention to the details of the fireplace moldings, the pattern in the china and the cuttings of the crystal.

"Mary, come out on the stoop and take a look here," Tom said.

She watched him through the screen as he sat on the top step and swept the space beside him with his hand. Mary took off her apron and hung it on a hook.

She stepped out, he patted the area and she sat down. Tom laid his arm across her shoulders and drew her close to him.

"Would anyone back in Ireland believe this? From a squalor in New York City amongst the filth, we now rise before the chickens to get on with the tasks of managing our magnificent land."

"I still have to pinch meself at times," she said.

"By the way, some of the lads haven't taken too kindly to the idea of Murdock being gone and me being in charge. I'm afraid I've had to let a couple of them go, and I've hired some new help."

"Who's that over there?" she asked.

Tom waved to a man leading a couple of horses from the stables. He did not acknowledge Tom's gesture and continued on.

"That's Sam, and he just happened to show up at the right time. Sam's as strong as a bull, keeps to himself and knows horses. So far, it looks like he's going to work out. Oh, and he's from Ireland to boot."

"Tom, I need to talk with you about Madame. As you know, she hasn't been eating well of late, and her cough is becoming quite harsh. I've called for Doc Everett to come by and look in on her."

"Don't you go worrying your wee self. He knows her well and will get to the bottom of this."

"Aye, Doc does at that," she said while eyeing Sam.

~

Madame's glassy eyes desperately searched the room. Sharp, rattling coughs persisted. She clutched her chest and struggled to catch her breath.

"It's tuberculosis. I'm sure of it, Mary."

"Doc Everett said you have pneumonia. Try to rest, Madame. You have a fever and you're very weak. We'll have another go at some tea and honey when you wake up."

Mary tucked a light blanket around her. Madame looked up with a pleading look in her eyes. "Please don't let them take me to the sanatorium, Mary. I want to be here at Avonvale just as you promised."

Mary sat beside her and patted her hand. "You'll always be at Avonvale with us. This is your home, and I'll take good care of you, Catherine."

Mary felt she witnessed an air of tranquility wave across Madame's face as she closed her eyes. Her tense limbs gave way sinking into the featherbed, and a restful smile crossed her dry, cracked lips.

"Thank you for planting our roses, Mary. You know how I love red roses," she whispered.

Mary looked over at the vase of white and cream roses on the bedside table. "You're welcome, Madame."

~

The next day, Mary entered Madame's bedroom carrying a silver tray. "Bonjour, Madame. I have your lemon verbena and a warm croissant."

Mary set the tray on a serving cart, poured the tea, inserted a wooden dipper into the honey pot and swirled the stick. "It's tea time in Paris," she said raising her voice a bit.

Mary returned the dipper and carried the tea to Madame's bedside table. She looked down at her. Madame's face was as pale as an opal, and her lifeless expression spoke clearly that she would never take another breath. Mary smoothed the coverlet and sat down. She laid Madame's hands one on top of the other, resting them on her stomach, and then she placed her hand on top of them.

"It's been delightful knowing you, Catherine. We'll lay you to rest behind our rose garden."

Mary spent this precious time with her friend sipping lemon verbena.

Chapter 23

The Promise

(1927)

It had been twelve years since the birth of their daughter, Anna. She was a bright and spirited girl who Tom felt was more than the daughter of Protestant Irish immigrants. She represented the future of this family.

Mary was his love and Anna, his joy.

Tom stood at the paddock railing. "Take Warrior around the ring again, but this time try jumping the low hurdles we set up. Check your alignment and heels down, Lass. He'll work with you."

Tom watched his daughter with intense scrutiny, his eyes locked on the team as they cleared three of the five jumps.

"Mind what you're doing, Anna. He's throwing his head again, and that'll cost you another penalty at competition."

Anna reined her horse to begin again, and they cleared all five. They walked the ring, and she saluted as she passed her father.

"That was grand. Now, cool him down. It'll soon be time for supper." Tom walked away, a smile curling his lips.

∾

Tom strolled past Mary and sat under the gazebo. He waved for her to join him.

Mary raised a hand to shade her eyes. "And what might you be doing in here?"

Tom removed an envelope from his trousers and laid it on the bench next to him.

"What's this?"

"Have a sit."

"There's nothing written on the front," she said.

"Go on, open it," he said with a smug little smile.

Mary opened the flap, removed a paper and unfolded it. Two passenger tickets fell to the ground.

Tom handed them to her. "I know how fierce you've missed your family and how hard it's been for you. You're going to Ireland, and this time you won't be traveling in steerage."

Tears welled up in her eyes. "They still want to see us?"

"Aye, they do. They'll all be there to meet you and their granddaughter at Belfast Harbor. The second ticket is for her. Sure I'll miss you both, but we have three mares soon to foal, and you might tell them I needed to stay behind to look after all this."

Her eyes followed his arm circumnavigating the one-hun-dred-twenty acres as if to hold it in the palm of his hand.

"I saw to it that Anna's passport is in order, and you'll have a week to get ready. I'll go with you next time."

A lone tear broke loose and drifted down Mary's cheek. She caught it with the edge of her finger and swept it away. Mary held out her arms to him, and Tom took her in his own. His embrace was gentle and endearing.

"I hardly know what to say except I wish you could come, too," she said. "Thank you, not just for this but for everything."

"Me gut said you'd agree, so you best run off and tell Anna. Sure she'll be packing her fanciest party dresses for the trip. You'll both be traveling in fine style."

~

When Mary and Anna returned from Ireland, Mary could barely contain herself. "Tom, everyone marveled over the newspaper articles featuring Avonvale. Our families are so proud for all you've accomplished. And, of course, they adored Anna."

"Me dad. What did *he* say?"

Mary took his hand and looked into his eyes. She sighed. "I'm so sorry. Your dad passed away. Your mum planned to tell you when you went over."

Tom bowed his head and finger-combed his hair back. "He died taking with him unsettled feelings for me. Taking you and our unborn baby away was the shame he surely never got over."

Mary paused. "That's not true, Tom. Before he died, she told me he forgave you."

Tom kissed her on the forehead. "Well, the horses won't feed themselves. I best tend to them."

~

Late that evening, Tom walked through the front door and tossed his cap on the hall rack.

"You look tired," Mary said. "After you wash up, why don't you meet me in the parlor. I've something to show you."

Mary returned with her hands behind her back.

Tom leaned in closer. "And just what are you hiding there?"

"Pick a hand," she said.

He pointed to her right hand, and Mary produced a brown felt fedora with a black grosgrain ribbon band.

"Let's see if it suits you," she said.

Mary pulled the ottoman over, stood on it and set the hat on his head.

Tom reached up and tipped it to one side. `

"Now, that's class if I do say so meself," she said.

～

Over time, Tom traded in a portion of his good nature for a stern and stiff upper lip. Back-to-back horse shows, auctions and managing their business as a top breeder replaced long evening walks with Mary and carriage rides with Anna.

The door swung open, and Tom stomped into the house. "Mary, where's your daughter?"

"She's gone dress shopping in Rochester with some friends. The All County Dance is coming up in a fortnight."

"She knew I needed her to go with me, and besides, she's too young to go to a dance."

"Well, if you'll remember, when I was about her age, I was crossing the pond with me husband to be."

"Well, I'm going to be bloody late. The horses are loaded, and I'm ready to go. She's getting too full of herself, and I'm not going to put up with her hijinks. It's a good thing she's not entered to ride. I'll have to grab one of the lads and deal with her later."

Mary stood on the porch and watched him storm off. "She's got a mind of her own, and I wonder who she got that from," she called out.

He looked back at her with a sheepish grin.

Chapter 24

Retribution

"I'm off to the auction," Tom announced. "Some fine thorough-breds are being brought in from Saratoga. Won't you join me, Mary? We'll get some peaches on the way back. I heard the Carricks out at Sugarberry still have some left."

"No doubt you'll be going on with business matters after and me roses need tending to. I'll whip up some biscuits and sweet cream for the peaches."

Tom stopped and faced her, lightly tracing the line of her collarbone with his finger. "That sounds grand."

He leaned forward and gently brushed the hair back from her face. In an instant, his lips were on hers. "I won't be long with business matters."

Mary's eyes lingered on him taking leave. Tom returned a tilt of his fedora.

~

Another pair of watchful eyes followed the pickup until it was out of sight. Sam stepped from the trees. A shadow fell across Mary's smile when she saw him.

He sauntered toward her, a cigar clenched between his teeth. "Ye better put your back into it for a mighty storm is coming." Sam snorted and waved a dismissal as he scuffled up The Green Road.

Mary clipped the last of her garden's blooms. She inhaled deep through her nose and thought autumn's air smelled crisp and cold some days, damp and earthier on others. It was her favorite season, and combined with the sun's warmth blanketing her body, Mary remembered her mum refer to autumn as "the second spring when every leaf is a flower, the hush before winter."

By late afternoon a cloud bank moved in, and the wind picked up changing its course as it flit through the leaves of the fir trees. A light, cool mist swept across Mary's face. She gathered the tools in her bushel basket and walked over to the gazebo. She sat on Madame's bench and watched a storm pass to the south. Distant thunder rumbled across the sky and flashes of silent lightning bounced between the clouds. Soon, the sun returned and brought with it a rainbow.

Mary looked up at the sky. "Madame, is that you bringing me such lovely colors over Avonvale?"

She followed the arch to its end and saw Sam tottering down the road. He loomed closer, his hands in his pockets. Mary pretended to ignore him at first; but as he drew nearer, she couldn't ignore the nauseous odor of stale cigar smoke wet with whiskey. Twin creases pinched the bridge of her nose, and she scrambled to her feet as he rounded the gazebo. His fingers drummed along the rail. A smoldering gaze spread across his face.

Mary held the pruning shears in front of her and glared into his eyes. "You best turn yourself around and head for the bunkhouse from where you came. Me husband is due back, and he'll not be taking kindly to the likes of you smelling up me lovely roses."

Sam sneered through a one-cornered smile. "Oh, really? I think it'll be a mighty while before we see the likes of him back here."

His gruff voice sounded as though it had been put through a meat grinder. He moved closer. "You know this is our moment, don't you."

Mary jumped back and waved the shears. Her mouth was set in a hard line. "No, it's not."

A frown swept across his face as he looked around. He clenched his jaw. "And just what do you think you're going to do with those, Lass?"

Mary held the shears in the air and leered at him. "Get away from me."

"You challenging me, are you?" He put a finger to his lips, and then his face lit up as though he would burst a blood vessel.

Sam reached for the shears. Mary stumbled and thrust them into his arm. Wide-eyed and panting, she took a step backward, her voice shaky, almost a stutter.

"Your, your arm — those scars. I remember you now. You were on the *Cedric*." She felt a sudden chill rush through her veins.

Sam backhanded her across the face knocking Mary into the thorny bushes. He stood over her gazing down. Mary crossed her arms in front of her face. The throbbing pain she felt grew more intense and traveled along her jaw. He crouched down, his muddled, bloodshot eyes vacant and hard. Mary felt an unbearable nausea as his stinking breath waved over her.

"One word to your husband, and you'll all wish you never stepped foot on Avonvale land." His voice was clipped and filled with dark rage.

Mary pushed herself up on one elbow and watched him stumble back up The Green Road. Shaking, she tried to stand, but her trembling leg buckled, and she rolled to one side. Mary soon heard Tom coming up the drive.

~

"I'm home with the peaches, and I've a grand surprise for Anna. Come and feast your eyes on her new thoroughbred. What do you say we call him Dreamaker. He'll fly over the jumps, Mary."

Tom opened the door and stepped inside. "I've a fierce thirst."

He turned on the faucet and reached for a glass. Beyond the kitchen window, Tom discovered Mary on her hands and knees in the middle of her rose garden. The door slammed behind him. He ran across the yard, his heart knocking against his ribs.

Tom reached down, and she winced at his touch as he helped her up. "Mary, what's happened to you?"

She looked up at him revealing a severely swollen cheek and deep, bloody scratches sweeping along the sides of her face. Her chin trembled like a small child.

"Sam came to me garden. He'd been in the drink. He grabbed me, and I stabbed him with me pruning shears."

As soon as she said the words, Tom's skin flushed hot and he clenched his jaw. He gently turned back her collar revealing more thorny punctures across her shoulders. Red seeping blotches, as abrasive as sandpaper, covered both hands. Mary shuddered.

Tom's mouth was a tight red knot. He felt raw inside, almost short of breath, but he spoke with a calm, controlled manner. "Did he do anything else to you?"

Salty drops fell from her chin, and she shoved air from her chest so she could speak. She shook her head. "No".

Tom helped her over to the gazebo. She sobbed into his chest, and he held her as tears soaked his shirt.

"Will you be alright here? This won't take long."

Mary nodded, and with staggered breathing, she clutched his arm. "He was on the boat. I remember the scars on his arm when he was crossing himself. Do you think he's been following us all this time?"

Tom eased her down on the bench and looked toward the bunkhouse with piercing eyes. His rage escalated with each heavy stride. Sam was passed out on a bunk, one arm dangling to the floor and the other wrapped in a bloody rag. An empty bottle of whiskey laid on the bed, a wool blanket drinking the last few drops.

He dragged Sam outside and dropped him to the ground. Hoisting him up by his collar, Tom drew his fist back like an arrow, taut and still, ready to be released. A fury he had never known came over him.

Mary called out, "Tom, stop!"

He released the barely conscious man and looked down at him, his eyes hard as flint.

"You've got five minutes to get the hell off this property. You'll never work in these parts again."

Once Tom was beyond earshot, Sam gurgled a few scant words deep in the bowels of his throat. "I'm not finished with you, Prot."

Chapter 25

You, Forever

Spring arrived bringing with it a cold, clear wind that whipped the sky blue and left behind air that was softer and warmer than it had been in months. Sun drenched sheets snapped on the line. Mary removed clothespins and collected them in her apron pockets. She looked beyond to the gazebo and her unattended rose garden. A cold chill ran up her spine.

Mary looked away as thoughts of Sam's attack threatened to taunt her. She spotted Anna's bicycle leaning against the shed. Mary marched over, knotted her skirt to one side and straddled the bike. "I believe our roses need tidying, Madame."

She pushed off and teetered down The Green Road, her feet atop one another on the frame and her mind in the dance of balance.Mary's excitement escalated as she sped across the lawn and through the thickets of low lying thorny plants. She tilted her face to the sun and let out a yip.

Tom looked on from across the yard. A small smile crossed his lips.

~

Tom sat on the porch steps. Mary stood beyond the screen door and watched him swipe away some acorns laying next to him. He looked up at her and stroked the beard stubble along his chin. The softness in his eyes accompanied a boyish grin that always defined Tom, no matter his age, she thought. His deep voice carried a serious tone, and sometimes he looked to be seven feet tall to her. She followed the contours of his strong arms and prominent, angular jaw.

Mary joined him carrying two stouts. "Here's a cold one for you, your Lordship." She curtsied and sat down.

"Thank you, me Lady." He gave a glimmer of a smile. "Do you see what we've got here, Mary?"

"Aye, but why don't you tell me anyway," she said.

"You're looking at the most prestigious equine center in the Finger Lakes Region, and we did it together."

Tom and Mary raised their bottles and toasted, "Slainte."

The sun waned through the trees and cast shadows that flickered across the lawn. Daylight came to a close.

AVONVALE

PART TWO

"Faith is the daring of the soul to go further than it can see."

~ OSCAR WILDE

Chapter 26

Across An Ocean Of Dreams

Andrew Wiley lived in Monkstown, Ireland, a village on an estuary of the River Lee. Winding dirt roads and thatched-roof cottages partnered with stone walls and boulders enclosing multi-shaded green fields like frames around artwork. Andrew's father, Ned, carved out a living as the local transporter carting potatoes, fish, wool and millet for the thresher.

Andrew breathed the earthy smell of grain and dusty hay that permeated throughout the timbers of his father's barn. Dim pallors of light streamed through the hewn beams creating a curtain of tiny particles that floated over the shapes of wood stalls and poles.

"Da, I decided I want to train with show horses some day. I've been reading about it, and I could start out as a stable hand at one of the farms in Kildare and become a work rider to begin with."

Silence ensued for what seemed like an eternity to Andrew. He could feel his heartbeat as they led the work horses into their stalls.

Ned looked at him with a hard stare which turned into a soft smile. "Well, it's more than you think, but if that's your dream, then make it happen, Lad. First off, you'll need start up money for room and board to get by before you're hired on. So how to come by that is the question."

Ned stepped into the isle and raised his finger in the air. "Have you ever taken a good look at Finn? He's different from the other horses here. He's even more than he appears, and I think I have an idea that'll work."

He walked outside, sat against the shed and pushed back the brim of his cap. Andrew sat beside him. Fascinated, he soaked in his father's unfeigned enthusiasm.

"I'll tell you the legend of Finn, a story mind you, a true story at that. Me mate, Murphy, was a stable boy at the manor of his Lordship Bradshaw. Within the confines of that stable was the blackest and fastest horse in the counties of Cork, Kerry and Tipperary all put together. That horse could put the grease on greased lightning and made Lord Bradshaw a very wealthy man." Ned removed his cap and beat off the dust against his leg.

"One morning, while Lord Bradshaw was off to an auction, I drove one of our young mares to his farm. Murph led the black stallion to a pasture behind the barns where our mare was in terrible heat. The stallion mounted her. Sure there were terrible noises of flicking and flacking, and the deed was done. I kept me fingers crossed that a great foal would come out of it. And behold, eleven months later, out popped Finn." Ned slapped his leg and chortled.

"As you can see, Finn has some black on him which is a nod to his father and a mane the color of the beach like his mother.

owner. He'll surely give you a job. A few of their riders have even competed at Madison Square Garden."

Andrew's eyes widened. Ned didn't flinch.

"I'll wire ahead, if you like."

"Sounds like a grand idea to me," Ned said. "What do you think, Andrew?"

"But, Da, I can't leave you and Ma here."

"Let's ride into Cork together," Ned said. "I want to show you something. There's still enough of the day in it." Ned tipped his cap. "Thank you, John. We'll get back to you."

At Cork Harbor, Ned looked into his son's eyes. "There's nothing for you here, Lad. I don't think a chance like this will come around again. Besides, I know you'll find your way to Madison Square Garden if you go. Now, that's a dream worth working for. The choice is yours."

They looked up at a stream of flags snapping in the wind from the towering main mast. "It's as if they're calling out orders for you to get underway," Ned said.

Andrew hugged his father. "Thank you, Da."

"Well then, the facts are clear. Let's get your papers in order and a ticket to America."

Andrew and his father stood with their arms across each other's shoulders and gazed at the sun barely above the horizon. Its light skewed among the clouds still vibrant and alive until it gradually melted into the sea.

"I'll be back for you and Ma," Andrew said.

"I know you will, Lad."

~

Andrew strained to focus through a dense early morning fog hanging over the harbor and draping the entrance to massive cement formations as the *Caledonia* approached Ellis Island. The imposing ship's stacks spewed black smoke of boiler steam and engine exhaust. Andrew looked over his shoulder at the large glowing sun. It began to move into the sky as if to own it, gradually illuminating the shore and unveiling this strange world of giant structures and his sanguine dreams. It crawled up the Statue of Liberty magnifying this long-awaited sight to behold. It's as if she's welcoming us to America, he thought.

Once ashore, some were greeted by family who had come before them but most, as was for Andrew, were complete strangers. He cut his way against a tide of bewildered and curious immigrants. He boarded a bus that traveled down Eighth Avenue, beyond Pennsylvania Station's Sports arena and one block west passing Madison Square Garden.

Chapter 27

New Life

Silhouettes of white belly osprey, with long narrow wings and long legs, flew across a chalky mauve and pale magenta sky. Andrew slept, his head resting against the window, the sun warming his face. When he opened his eyes, the bus was snaking through a lush green valley spattered with cornfields as far as he could see. A river ran alongside the land where horses grazed.

The bus approached a roundabout in the Village of Avon and pulled over to the side of the road. Andrew's attention was drawn beyond a cornfield where a figure cantered upon a spirited bay.

From his window seat, Andrew's heart leapt with the horse as it cleared stone walls and split rail fences with ease and grace.

"Son! This is the end of the line for you," the driver called out.

Andrew moved to the front of the bus and got off.

She stood in the stirrups and waved. Andrew waded through towering stalks, sweeping them apart. All the rider could see were brown tassels diving around him as his movements continually narrowed the distance between them. She noticed the sounds of a commanding breeze pushing through the field and outweighing the hum of distant motor traffic. In the shade of her hand, she looked for him to appear and nudged her horse to move closer.

Andrew stumbled out, brushed himself off and shook the corn silk from his tousled black hair. His light blue eyes sloped down at the corners giving him a look of innocence. A playful smile etched its way back into his face. He chuckled under his breath. "Could your cornfield be just a might bigger?"

She heard herself gasp, hoping he didn't. Reining her horse in a circle, she snapped her head around to prolong eye contact. Her short-cropped hair, framing high cheekbones, seemed to bounce as her horse pranced in place. She wasn't accustomed to her confident nature being challenged, but the sight of him moved her heart to a place it had never been before. She leaned forward and extended her hand. "I'm Vivian Collins, and this is Achilles."

He grinned. "I'm Andrew Wiley. Might the Clements farm be nearby?"

She pointed to a distant redbrick mansion and remained captivated for what seemed to her like an awkward eternity.

Andrew broke the silence. "I'm from Ireland." He rubbed the back of his neck.

"So you're the Irishman Mr. Connaty called about. Mr. Clements is expecting you. Hop on; we'll take you there."

Andrew grabbed his backpack and swung up behind her.

"You better hang on tight just in case he takes off."

Vivian squeezed the horse with her legs and clicked her tongue. Andrew jolted back and grabbed her around the waist. The corners of her mouth ticked up as they cantered across the field.

∾

"Tom, Mary, this is Andrew Wiley. I found him wading through my cornfield."

Andrew reached out his hand and shook Tom's. "Thank you for seeing me Mr. Clements."

"What part of Ireland are you from, Lad?"

"Monkstown in County Cork, Sir."

"We're from County Antrim, and you're just in time for supper." Mary said.

Tom nodded. "Join us, Lad."

Andrew pulled out a chair for Vivian. She blushed and sat down.

The eight-foot-long table was draped with an exquisite white linen and lace tablecloth. A baroque mirror reflected the highly polished candelabra in the center. An oil painting of a fox hunt at dawn hung at one end of the room. Andrew thought of home and the old kitchen table that wobbled.

Mary served nettle soup, leg of lamb with mint jelly, russet potatoes, turnips and crusty brown bread. Andrew smelled bread pudding with currants baking and remembered his mother saying it smelled like cinnamon-vanilla heaven.

"Tom and Mary have a daughter, Anna," Vivian said. "She's at the University of Pennsylvania, and she'll be home for the holidays."

"Oh Vivian, I haven't told you that Anna is going to be taking an internship over the holidays," Mary said. "She decided to free up her summer and spend it training with Dreamaker."

Tom leaned forward, his elbows resting on the table. "So what brought you across the pond, Andrew?"

"Me da is a transporter and mostly carts crops for farmers to the market. Ma would go with him and sell her breads and rolls until me sister died after falling down a steep bank. Ma was so sad that she just stopped doing all the things she loved."

Andrew bowed his head and took a slow breath. "Da said it was like a suffocation of her spirit."

Mary blotted the corners of her mouth with her napkin. "I'm so sorry, Andrew."

"Anyway, I read some books about training horses, and after graduating secondary school, I told me da I wanted to be a horse trainer." Andrew shrugged. "Da thought it was a grand idea, so he entered me and our horse, Finn, in our county's harvest festival race after we trained over the summer."

The more Andrew talked, the more enamored Vivian became with him. She leaned in closer. "And you won, right?"

Andrew broke into a wide smile. "Aye, we did, and the payoff was mighty good since we ran 10-1."

"Bravo!" she blurted.

"I was offered a job to train in Ireland and also in America. Da said if I want to follow me dream, it will be in America. Next thing I knew, he bought me a ticket and wouldn't take no for an answer."

Andrew looked suddenly pensive. "When I have enough money saved, I'm sending for them, and Da will never need to work again."

"I believe you will, Andrew," Mary said.

Andrew tugged at his collar. "But when I got here, no job was waiting. So I worked at a couple of farms harvesting crops and helping with barn chores until Mr. Connaty told me about Avonvale. He said you're looking for help in your stables and care of your horses."

Tom took a last bite of dessert and pushed back from the table. "We surely are, and that's quite a story, Lad. The day begins at six-thirty."

"Breakfast is at six," Mary said.

Chapter 28

Purple Rain

Andrew's responsibilities included grooming and exercising several horses each day in addition to his stable chores. Vivian and Andrew also rode together whenever possible. Her degree in equine studies included the art of dressage, and she instructed Andrew in the refined movements of rhythm and balance, a synchronization that soon took horse and rider jumping over low fences with ease.

"Andrew, I'll help you with the barn chores. Time got away from us in the arena today, and Mary will be serving dinner soon," Vivian said.

"You don't have to do that. It won't take me long."

"I insist."

Andrew handed her a pitchfork. "Let's get to it then."

He started to muck out a stall. Vivian did the same, her eyes full of playfulness as she continued to admire his strong back and shoulders.

"Vivian, do you.mind me asking how you and the Clementses became such good friends?"

"I don't mind. Actually, the cabin where I live belonged to my parents. When I was six, they were killed in a car accident. Tom and Mary took me in, and they have always treated me like a daughter. Anna has been like a kid sister to me. After I graduated from college, I decided to move back to the cabin and, you know, just have a place of my own. That's the short version."

Vivian rounded the end of the stall, put her arms around his neck, leaned in close and they held a kiss.

"I love you, Andrew."

He placed his hands on her shoulders.

"I'm sorry, Vivian."

Vivian's face flushed, and she bit her lip to stave off the tears. "You have nothing to be sorry for. I shouldn't have said that."

"Still friends?" Andrew said with sullen eyes.

"Of course, we are." She turned away. "I'm going to see if I can help Mary with dinner."

～

Spring brought with it the warming sun and bird songs announcing the summer. Tom appeared at the gable door. "Might I have a word with you, Andrew?"

"Aye, Mr. Clements." Andrew pulled a bandana from his pocket and wiped his face and neck.

"I see you've been training on Vivian's horse in your spare time. You take a fine seat, Lad."

Andrew's eyebrows rose a notch.

"I'm soon bringing on more help and would favor you spending most of your time training with Dreamaker. I'd like to see how you two work together."

Tom removed his fedora and re-shaped the crown to a deeper crease. "If that suits you, of course."

A broad smile spread across Andrew's face. "Yes, Sir. It suits me just fine."

"Very well then. We'll see how it goes." Tom placed the hat back on his head and adjusted it to his liking before walking away.

Vivian remained around the corner. The ash at the end of her cigarette curled and stretched like a scorched snake.

Chapter 29

Ever I Loved You

Tom met Anna at the train station late in May. He drove in silence absorbing every word that spilled from her mouth. She had his heart in her pocket from the day she was born. Anna's enthusiasm was contagious, and Tom thought how grand it will be to have her home for the summer.

Anna peered up at the majestic arched sign that introduced Avonvale.

"The conifers seem taller than ever."

"Aye, nothing stays the same," Tom said. "Just look at you, all grown before me very own eyes."

Anna rolled down her window. She breathed in the subtle, sweet fragrances of her mother's roses. Along with the earthiness of the approaching stables, she embraced this welcome mat.

Anna eyed the widow's walk and cupola, her childhood sanctuary, which allowed her to view the surrounding valley. It was her favorite place to escape. She remembered the excitement she felt when the majesty of lightning and thunder crashed around her on those wild stormy days. The night's gifts revealed secrets of a million stars like fireflies floating against its pitch-black backdrop

"Father, who is that riding Dreamaker?"

"That would be Andrew Wiley. He's been working with Dreamaker while you've been away. Vivian volunteered to train with them."

Anna toyed with a lock of her hair. "Vivian looks quite captivated by him."

Tom continued to look ahead. "I told you about Andrew. He's also been a mighty help around here especially since I got rid of that no good git."

Anna leaned forward and turned her face to him. "Why did you fire Sam, Father?"

Tom continued to look ahead. "Some things just don't need answering."

"Anyway, I got the impression that Andrew is just a stable hand," she said.

Tom laughed under his breath. "Well, he's more than that, but he doesn't hold a candle to you in the arena." He winked at her. "Welcome home, Lass."

Her adoring smile lingered as they pulled alongside the paddock.

Anna stepped from the truck. Her auburn hair was pinned up on the sides and long waves cascaded down her back. Her delicate ivory skin was a nod to her Irish heritage, and her petite frame was also a nod to Mary.

Andrew lost all concentration when he saw her and his balance shifted. Dreamaker tossed his head up at the approaching jump, bolted sideways and Andrew was on the ground. Vivian rushed over as he leapt to his feet and brushed himself off.

"Are you alright?" Vivian asked, unable to gain eye contact with him.

"Aye. Is that Anna?"

His eyes were drinking her in. Grinning, he casually began walking over to Tom and Anna.

Vivian waved above her head. "Welcome home!" She averted her eyes as she passed Andrew handing him off the reins. "Wait here."

Anna and Vivian greeted each other with a hug.

"So how did your exams go? Have you met anyone special yet, or are you still keeping them guessing?"

"Neither one. Actually, I've been just too busy for any of that."

Vivian folded her arms and rolled her eyes. "Right, and I'm the Queen of England."

"Give me some time with Mother, and then how about we go for a ride and catch up."

"Sounds good. That'll give me time to groom Dreamaker and saddle up a couple other horses."

"Oh, is Andrew too tired to do that?"

"You are certainly in fine form your first day back," Vivian said.

Tom grabbed Anna's luggage, and they disappeared into the house. Once inside, Tom turned and noticed Vivian walking over to Andrew with a stiff gait. He closed the door behind him.

Vivian snatched the reins from Andrew and walked toward the stables. Midway, she stopped and spun around.

"By the way, yes, that's Anna."

"I'll cool Dreamaker down," he said.

"You better cool yourself down, Romeo," she said under her breath.

Horse in tow, Vivian disappeared around the back side of the stables. She's here just for the summer, and then she'll be going back, she thought. After all, when it comes down to it, Anna can get any man she wants. Surely she isn't about to settle for someone without the high pedigree she's accustomed to. Vivian lit a cigarette and sucked in a lungful.

∾

Andrew led Dreamaker from the stables early one morning. The sun introduced its golden light over the glistening dew-ladened meadow. He looked over to see Anna approaching. She wore highly polished riding boots and walked with an easy fluid grace.

"Oh, you're training with Dreamaker," she said.

"I didn't know you had plans to ride this morning. How about you take Dreamaker. I'll saddle up the dapple-gray and join you."

Andrew handed Anna the reigns and disappeared inside. He returned carrying a two-step mounting block.

"This might help," he said.

Anna avoided his gaze, stepped up, gripped the pommel and easily mounted her horse before shortening the stirrups.

"We'll be at the north paddock," she said with an engaging smile.

She reined her horse around, and as Dreamaker loped across a field of clover and wild flowers, the attraction she felt for Andrew multiplied.

~

By late summer, the soft brushing sounds of wheat fields, like surf on a yellow sea, became a steady crackle as the grains were now golden and dry. Strong breezes swept about causing wave-like effects on a humid afternoon. Vivian saddled up and rode over to the Clements's farm. Mary was watering her roses.

"Mary, do you know where Anna is? I thought she might like to take a ride."

"Aye, she and Andrew went down to the creek to collect the last of the fiddleheads for supper. They should be back soon. You'll be joining us, won't you?"

"Sounds good to me, thank you. I think I'll ride over and give them a hand."

Aware of her infatuation for Andrew, Mary felt that Vivian would have been safer amidst the thorns of her rose bushes.

~

Entering the woods, Achilles stepped gingerly through the tall trees. Vivian heard no one and assumed they had ventured to the other side of the creek. She kept a tight rein, and before long, she heard Anna's delicate laughter. Vivian felt a sting in the back of her eyes as she focused on Andrew and Anna laying in each other's arms along the bank. Her heart plummeted.

She remembered the taste of his grin the day he stepped out of her cornfield at dusk. It was the day she invited an Irishman to feast upon her heart. Vivian vowed she would never allow herself to feel that way again.

Chapter 30

The Garden

The winter's white blanket had come and gone, hydrating the meadows of Avonvale. Andrew and Anna were married in April when the awakening wisteria blooms and rosebuds graced their wedding day beneath Madame's gazebo. Anna wore her grandmother's wedding veil.

~

Over that summer, Andrew and Dreamaker hit the horse show circuit with gusto. Their focus pointed toward more and more championships at significant area events.

"Andrew, Joseph will be taking over your chores. Your work with Dreamaker is to be first and foremost leading up to the National Horse Show," Tom said.

"What are you talking about?"

"Why, Madison Square Garden, of course."

Andrew's eyes widened and he beamed as he recalled his father's words. "I know you'll find your way to Madison Square Garden. Now that's a dream worth working for."

"Andrew, I'll be needing you to go ahead of me with Dreamaker. I'm giving you the reins," Tom said.

"Don't you have to be there as the owner?"

"Meet me on the porch. I'll be right along," Tom said.

Tom appeared through the back door and handed Andrew some papers.

"You can read through these, but I'll tell you first off that all you really need to do is sign your name on the dotted line. And if you do, you'll be part owner of Dreamaker. I'm needed here to take care of a few matters, so we'll join you in a couple days."

Tom offered Andrew a pen. "Do we have a deal, Son?"

Andrew stretched out his hand with a big smile. "Yes, sir!"

Tom reached out to Andrew with both arms.

∾

Finally, autumn arrived and with it, the National Horse Show at Madison Square Garden, the grandeur pageantry of *mink and manure.*

Andrew awoke in an exquisite room at the Wyndham Garden Hotel. He walked down a grand English oak staircase leading to the lavish main lobby. He could hear the faint murmur of a fountain as well as the soft tinkling of jewels and rustling silk gowns as women glided across the highly polished marble tiles.

Crowds of hotel guests whirled through its revolving brass and glass doors. Andrew waited for an opening and exited to the right. Several taxis lined the curb.

A driver called out. "Where you goin'?"

"Madison Square Garden."

"Jump in; I'll take you there."

Andrew imagined the taxi driver to have a face that was pure New York, pointed and intent like that of a falcon. He started the meter and they drove off.

～

The riding events were scheduled for five consecutive days. Andrew felt confident that Dreamaker demonstrated the consistency and stamina of a champion. He made it to the finals and was tied in the Open Jumper Division. For their jump-off on that last day, the course was long and intricate. It wove around the Garden oval in four overlapping loops. It included quick turns and changes of direction, combinations that called for perfect timing and coordination. Whether it was the tenseness of the moment, the wear and tear from days of competition or the difficulties of the course, no one could be sure. At any rate, his counterpart knocked down the last barrier.

It was up to Dreamaker to run a clean course. He began to sidestep and toss his head.

"Let's do this for Tom and Mary," Andrew whispered. Dreamaker crescendoed up to the first jump, and the big seventeen-hander exploded over it, over the triple bar jump, the chicken coop, the hog's-back, the bull's eye and the striped panel. They had developed a rhythm and relaxation that stilled and captivated all who were in attendance. Their synchronization was flawless, and as they thrust forward over the final jump, Dreamaker's graceful arc was clean and it was done.

～

Cameras flashed from every direction in the winner's circle. It was a momentous time they would always cherish. For Mary, equally as memorable was when she heard a woman say her name. She turned around and there stood Gracey.

"Donnie was in Kilcullens. Imagine that," she nervously sniggered. "Says a bloke saw that Tom Clements entered a horse in the big leagues here."

"Gracey, this is me daughter, Anna." Mary took Gracey's hand, and her words leapt out. "Anna, this is me dear friend, Gracey."

Mary and Gracey gazed at each other. Mary hugged her. "I love you, too, Gracey."

"And this is Anna's husband, our son, Andrew Wiley," Tom said.

The cloud cover was lifting and separating, revealing ribbons of watery blue sky. They stood in front of the arena. The sidewalks were alive with people weaving around them with hands gesticulating and expressions focused.

Andrew looked just three blocks up the street at the Wyndham Garden Hotel from where he took a thirty-minute taxi ride.

Chapter 31

Timeless Love

It was one of those early spring days with a kiss of coldness. From Mary's bedroom window she paused to notice the shade trees knitted together, their buds ready to open into the light, to be green flags in the ever-warming wind. It was a day simply for noticing.

~

Tom called from the bottom of the stairs. "Mary, might you be ready to go soon?"

"Aye, Tom. I'll be down straight away."

Mary stood before a full-length mirror and twirled once around. She felt like a girl again.

The half-light of dawn sifted through a stained glass window. Dots of prism colors sprayed the staircase. Mary rounded the curve of the railing and stopped at the second floor landing. Tom looked up and gazed upon the Irish girl he loved all through his life. A yellow chiffon dress clung to her small frame. It fluttered at the hem just below her knees as she elegantly walked down the stairs, her hand running along the rich mahogany rail.

"It's yellow," Tom said grinning.

The heightened color of her cheeks and her sparkling eyes spoke of the love she had always known with him.

"Someone once told me that yellow suits me. I made it meself, and I thought today might be a good day to wear it."

Tom knew this vision of her would forever remain embedded in his mind. He placed his hand on her back and escorted her to the door.

The farmer's market bustled with people shopping for seasonal homegrown fruits and vegetables, fresh eggs and local honey. Sausages and whole chickens hung above beds of ice displaying an array of fish and shellfish. Mouth watering cakes and pies infused with the vinegar smell of sour dough bread.

"The aromas are divine," Mary said.

"How about a fizzy and some scones. Me stomach's been rumbling, and that should hit the spot. Sound good to you?"

"It does, but might we sit down by the water where it's cooler?"

"Are you feeling all right, Mary?"

"This humidity is just after me. I'll be right as rain after a cold fizzy."

The branches of river birch trees intertwined along the bank providing a thick canopy of shade, and from somewhere a gentle breeze settled in. They sat on the soft underlying grass near a group of lush lavender and pink lilac trees in bloom. A sweet, heady scent surrounded them.

He raised her chin and pressed his lips to hers — a lingering, tender kiss.

"That was lovely," she said. "You know, for the most part you began to kiss me differently after we owned Avonvale."

Tom cocked his head. "I did, did I? Do tell me more."

"Well, perhaps it was the two of us focusing on the responsibilities of running our estate. Then Anna came along. You never neglected me, no never. But this last kiss took me back to our early years and that afternoon in the meadow."

"I've learned that something changes in a man when he owns land. It becomes a second love which perhaps affects the first," Tom said. "It was never intentional. At one point, I think I became more proud of you than feeling just a young man's love."

"You know I saw the same vision as you, Tom." Her eyes followed a family of ducks paddle through the water.

Tom turned her face to his and looked into her eyes. "I love you more now than I ever have."

Mary brushed her fingertips across his mouth. "I've always loved you, and I always will."

Tom stood, reached down and took her hands, pulling her into his arms.

～

When they arrived at Avonvale, Mary slipped off her shoes. "I'm still not feeling the best of me. I think I'll take a wee nap."

"I'll go up with you and open the window."

Their bedroom caught the late afternoon light. A bar of weak sunlight spread across the room. Mary closed her eyes.

Tom raised the window sash midway, covered her with the sheet and kissed her.

"Sweet dreams, me Lady."

Chapter 32

Dark Night Of The Soul

It was twilight, deep in September. The stables were stocked with dry, brittle hay. Andrew stood in the kitchen.

"Would you take a pint, Tom?"

"Too late to go to town," he replied with a chuckle.

"How'd you like it, poured or by the neck?"

Tom listened to the trill of a skylark, memories of Mary flooding his mind. "I'll take a jar."

Andrew pushed the screen door open with his foot and joined Tom on the porch. Mary had always lined the perimeter with several large hanging ferns and white wicker rockers. Anna continued the tradition after her mother's passing. Tom scanned the season's remains of Mary's rose garden. He bowed his head. "She mostly fancied the white ones. Always did."

He took out his pocket watch. "Where's Anna?"

"She's upstairs resting. The baby will be here in just a month or so," Andrew said.

Tom's attention took him to a damaged rose bush which Mary had asked him to replace. He meant to take care of it, but he got so involved with the threshing of the hay and all.

I'll have to do that, he thought.

∼

Dusk ebbed into evening. The first stars shined like sequins as they began their nightly dance. Full-length gold sheers ruffled to the command of a spirited breeze. Anna felt a chill, got up and walked over to close the window.

She turned her face to the big buttery moon. Anna felt it seemed to claim a vast peacefulness stretching across the valley. Its soft orange rays illuminated a path over the land and kissed her right cheek.

Anna noticed a figure standing along the fence which encompassed the stables.His arms laid atop the rail, bent at the elbows. He turned his face up to her bedroom window. She turned away and squeezed her eyes wondering if whom she saw was real or imaginary. When she looked back, he was gone.

There was not a sound but that of a barn owl calling his question through the dark night.

∼

Hours later, a serene stillness throughout the stables was broken. The strike of a match followed by a pungent, sulfurous odor permeated within the walls creating a heavy scent of scorched wood. The comforting dim lights flickered and then went dark. Restless horses and blackness joined searing flames crawling along its lethal path of destruction.

Everyone at Avonvale woke to the curdling screams of frantic horses. Beyond the front door, an inferno of revenge illuminated the sky with devastation. An angry fire, aided by hot, dry wind, tunneled throughout the stables, and the blaze continued to rise casting a foreign light over their valley.

"Andrew, get the men. Grab burlap sacks and throw them over the horses' heads. We got to get them out of there!"

Neighboring farmers sped across the fields and up the drive. Men and women filled buckets with water and formed a chain in an attempt to gain control of the relentless blaze. Frenzied horses reared and lunged against their stalls causing a deafening banging. Others bucked wildly, kicking their powerful hind legs and making it nearly impossible to help them escape from the growing flames of white-hot blue and saffron yellow.

Andrew ran to Dreamaker's stall and led him out to safety. The flames licked and curled around the gable doorframe of an adjoining stable. Heavy black smoke billowed across the rafters. Tom struggled to pull a gable door along its track. When it finally opened, a violent backdraft hurled him several yards across the grounds.

Vivian and Anna remained on the porch, holding each other, their bodies trembling.

Powerful flames rose higher and crackled fiercely. Andrew charged back into the inferno to rescue more horses trapped inside.

The others stayed behind with Tom and helplessly watched as the buildings neared collapse from a blaze that could now be seen for miles around.

Andrew looked over his shoulder to see that Dreamaker had followed him. He grabbed the horse's mane at the withers and pulled himself up. It was at that moment, the flaming, charred timber columns around them crumbled causing the roof to follow.

A haunting cry rose above the pandemonium. Tom called out to the Catholic Irishman who had become his beloved son.

Chapter 33

Remembrance

Tom sat in his wheelchair, lethargic and weak, his legs numb and scarred. Once a proud man of physical strength with a passion for life, he was now at the mercy of this icy metal apparatus to support his broken frame.

He sat at a window in Vivian's cabin which faced south. He viewed Avonvale, his treasured estate. It stood alone. The stables were gone.

He remembered stating many times, *Avonvale is our flag; she is our home, a gift to maintain.* A sharp feeling, sudden and strong, overcame him. They're all gone, he thought. My family. My horses. My life.

He reflected over the recent ruination of Avonvale. It was the fire that triggered a domino effect of catastrophes. He vaguely remembered being thrown from the stables, but he clearly remembered the roof collapsing on Andrew and Dreamaker. His eyes pinched shut, and he choked back the tears.

~

A chill ran through his veins as he recollected Vivian appearing at his bedside.

Hostile sounds, like that of heavy gurgled breathing, emanated from various life-saving machines. The monitor's continuous beep, beep, beep were his only roommates. Bright white lights bounced out at him, but he didn't know from where.

He remembered feeling the reality of death and the absence of his family.

"It was all so quick. Tom, Doc didn't get there in time so I delivered your granddaughter. She was premature but doing well now, and I've been calling her Andrea - after her father."

His furrowed brow deepened. "Where's me daughter?"

They looked into each other's eyes and he knew before Vivian spoke.

"Tom, you were badly burned and on high doses of morphine. You have been in and out of consciousness for almost two months." She laid her hand on his; her eyes looked tired and heavy.

"Andrew didn't make it either. I'm so sorry." Vivian drew a labored breath. "Pierre arranged to have them with Mary behind her rose garden."

~

Tom listened to the rain drum against the windows surrounding the large, open spaces of Vivian's cabin. Vivian's words rolled over and over in Tom's head. The sound of her voice had seemed so distant, like in a faraway place.

He reflected on Mary's gentle Irish lilt and sparkling eyes as they walked along the midway eating their first hot dogs. When he cupped her face in his hands and kissed mustard from the corner of her mouth, she later told him that it took her breath away. He thought of those passionate nights at the bungalow and their first night in the big house.

Tom closed his eyes. "What am I to do without you, Mary?"

Vivian walked over to him. "Can I do anything for you, Tom?"

Tom whirled his chair around. His face was tight and grave. "Aye, you can get me Mary, Anna and Andrew, me estate for starters and two good legs to boot!"

He lowered his head then looked up with knitted brows and red-rimmed eyes. "I'm so sorry, Vivian. I just don't know what I'm going to do without them."

"You can always remember the years at Avonvale being a place you felt you came out of the ground, the love you had with Mary and Anna, where you realized your dream and helped Andrew attain his."

Vivian leaned in closer. "You know, Tom, we never really own anything. There are no guarantees with the people in our lives, even our land, contrary to how much we sometimes want to believe differently." She hesitated. "I learned the hard way by fighting this very thought."

"You mean Andrew, right?"

It took her a moment to find her voice. "That's right, Tom, and you also know that I loved Anna."

"I know you did, Lass. I meant no harm."

"I know you didn't."

～

Tom sat at the window viewing his beloved Avonvale. More and more, this was where he generally found himself. The estate remained unoccupied. He remembered what his dad said so many years before about the land becoming a part of you — a responsibility you'll never want to leave. Tom sighed as he took in the gray clouds and pouring rain.

Andrea toddled up behind him and peeked around the side of his chair. "Boo!"

Tom jumped a little, and they both laughed. She reached around with her arms in the air. "Up."

Tom lifted her up on his lap and looked into her light blue eyes. He brushed wavy auburn locks from her face. She scrunched her nose, freckles splashed across her cheeks.

"Ah, you're the image of your mum and dad all put together. Surely you have a big heart to boot."

She nestled her head into his chest, and they watched the wind whip about the trees surrounding Avonvale.

"Wasat?"

"That's home, me dear."

She wriggled about, and he set her down. She pointed to a framed photo which caught the morning light. It was taken on Andrew and Anna's wedding day.

"That's our family, Lass."

Andrea blew him a kiss. He did the same, and she scampered away.

Tom reflected back to that unforgettable day.It was a time when we were all there — one of the happiest times in me life, he thought.

～

"Vivian, would you come in here and have a sit with me?"

She pulled over the ottoman and sat beside him. "I just put Andrea down for a nap. You have my undivided attention." Vivian sensed a peacefulness about Tom.

He rested his elbows on the arms of his chair and intertwined his fingers. "I have two requests of you as me days seem to be winding down." He leaned forward and faced her. "When me time comes, will you take legal guardianship of Andrea? You'll receive substantial funds to do so, and it will give me great comfort to know she'll be with you, especially as much as you loved Andrew and Anna."

Vivian lowered her head and rubbed the back of her neck. She nodded. "Yes, of course I will, Tom."

"And Vivian, promise me you'll often tell her all about her mother and father and our story of Avonvale. Will you do that for me?"

"You have my word."

"Very well. I'll make a call, and we'll draw up the papers."

A weight lifted from Vivian's shoulders. Raising Andrew's daughter was a way to always be in union with him. Vivian felt she could do this for Andrea while being supportive of her father's legacy. She could never have Andrew, but she would always have a part of him, and she would not let him down.

Chapter 34
The Green Road

A week later, Tom sat in his chair at the open front door and watched his attorney drive away.

Scattered leaves of warm gold, burnt oranges and sepia fluttered in the strengthening wind. Soft chocolaty browns also added to a comforting autumn quilt that stretched along the front lawn finalizing the season.

Vivian placed her hand on his shoulder. "There's a chill in the air. I made some chowder. What do you say we have some?"

Tom gazed across the cornfield. Dried cornstalks laid on the ground from the last cutting. His eyes were dull and listless.

"We'll never really know how the fire started, will we?"

"No, Tom, I don't believe we ever will."

～

Later that day, Tom turned the wheels of his chair and entered the kitchen. A warm breeze sifted through the screen door, and he braced it open with an elevated leg rest. Tom's adrenaline began to escalate. His aching arms became an extension of his will as he pushed harder and faster up The Green Road. However, his progress was abruptly halted when one of the wheels dipped into a rut and he spilled onto the path.

Tom rolled his head to the side; his face rested on the green center grasses that contained their fresh, clean scents along with the sweet aromas of tiny wild flowers. He breathed in the memories and was lulled back to the days in Ireland when he and Mary played as children and ultimately fell in love.

Tom closed his eyes. Mary slipped her dainty hand in his and he stood with ease. They walked together up The Green Road and soon transformed back to the young lovers they once were.

The song of a skylark and children's laughter resonated at the top.

AVONVALE

PART THREE

"My somber heart seeks you always."
~ Pablo Neruda

Chapter 35

New Beginning

Vivian took a drag from her cigarette, inhaled deeply, leaned forward and blew the smoke through the open vent window.

She glanced down at Andrea curled up beside her as she drove east. Vivian thought of her plan to move to a rural area of Worcester County, Massachusetts, which was now in full effect. Here, she would masquerade as a single mother at a place where they had no history. Her life as Andrew's widow could now begin.

~

Vivian snuffed out a cigarette with the toe of her riding boot and lit another. She took a hard drag, tossed her head back and blew the smoke into the air.

"You get one more ticket in that jalopy of yours for your heavy foot and I'll…"

"You'll *what* Mother?"

The tone with which Andrea said Mother carried a sarcastic note throughout her high school years. Vivian concluded that Andrea's overall personality was not warm and friendly toward anyone, for that matter, and so she chose to grin and bear it.

I can't tell her the truth, she thought. I can't risk how she would react. I want her to always be my daughter — Andrew's and mine.

∼

Andrea seldom came home while attending the University of Boston. Vivian would say she made rare cameo appearances, like a shooting star across a summer sky.

Andrea stepped on the accelerator, her ponytail snapping in the wind. As she sped along, she could make out someone leading her horse around the corner to the backside of the stables. She jumped from her car just as Vivian appeared at the entrance with a pleasing smile.

"Andrea, what a wonderful surprise, and you've actually got the top down today."

Andrea turned her cheek as Vivian stepped forward to give her a kiss.

"I thought you were going to the Hamptons this weekend."

"I changed my mind, too boring," she replied. "What happened to Scout? He's limping and who is that with him?"

"Matthew is the veterinarian taking over for Doc Haller. I told him he has some big shoes to fill."

Vivian leaned forward. Phlegmy, wet, crackling noises kicked up in her throat, and Andrea waited for another coughing fit to pass.

Matthew had circled around the stables and appeared from the other side.

"Vivian, are you all right? Is there anything I can do for you?"

Andrea took the halter as he helped Vivian over to a bench. "I'll get you some water."

Andrea stroked Scout's withers, nuzzled her face into his sleek neck and talked to him with a soft, loving tone. "What's going on, boy?"

Vivian couldn't help but notice Andrea's warm affection toward her horse. It was a side of her that Vivian had never seen before, not with anyone, and certainly not with herself.

Matthew walked over to Vivian with a cup of water.

She took a sip and cleared her throat to relieve the wheezing which invaded her more and more. "Thank you, Matthew. That's much better. In any case, I got a call from the Hannahs out at Dutch Hollow. They're expecting a breech with one of their mares, and I told Des you'd call him back."

"Would you mind calling him for me, and tell him I'll be there soon?"

"Not at all," Vivian said.

Andrea examined Scout's hoof and looked up at Matthew. "It appears he has an abscess."

"Scout has developed a mild case of laminitis," he said.

"Of course it is," Andrea said. "After all, you're the bona fide veterinarian."

"Andrea studied animal husbandry her freshman year at the university," Vivian said. "However, she switched her major on me and decided to become a writer."

"Looks like we got it early," Matthew said. "I gave him an antibiotic and something for pain. Andrea, he needs to stand in ice water; and since I have to go, I'm sure you can handle that, right?"

"Of course, I can." She shot him a cheesy smile.

"That's good news," Vivian said.

"By the way, it's better to be happy with your own choices than to settle for someone else's, don't you think, Mother?"

"Matthew, please join Andrea and me for my lemon roasted chicken after you get back from the Hannah's."

"I would like that," Matthew said. "Now, if you ladies will excuse me, I have another horse that needs my attention."

∼

Andrea clattered down the stairs and slowed at the second floor landing. "Where's my cap and gown, Mother?"

"In the vestibule closet. I had your gown dry cleaned and the cap is in a box on the shelf."

She nonchalantly walked down the last flight. "Of course, you did."

"We have to leave within the hour in order to find a good parking space. Please be ready."

Andrea popped the cap on her head and tossed her gown over the banister. It slid to the floor as she lumbered up the stairs, two at a time. Vivian walked over, picked up the gown and hung it back in the closet.

"Relax, Mother. This whole graduation thing will be over soon," she called out.

∼

Vivian slipped out the back door and fished out a pack of cigarettes from her purse. She shook one up, lit it and sucked in a lungful. She heard Andrea approaching, blew a cloud over her shoulder and extinguished it in a flower pot. Andrea stepped onto the porch wearing her graduation cap. Her gown draped over one shoulder, and she handed it to Vivian.

"Your lungs are going to turn black and rot away, you know."

"I'll be right back." Vivian disappeared in the house.

Andrea waited beside her mother's car as Vivian always locked it. Vivian returned with the gown on a hanger, handed it to her, opened the garage door and revealed a shiny red convertible.

"Let's take yours today," she said. "Congratulations, my dear."

"Oh, you shouldn't have, but thank you. It's flashy to say the least, and I don't want to be the envy of all my classmates. Would you mind driving yours? You understand."

Vivian swallowed hard. "Of course, my dear." She unlocked her car, and Andrea slid in the front seat. Vivian hung the gown in the back.

Vivian focused on the road, and Andrea sat vacant-eyed in the lacy, flickering sunlight that filtered through the branches of maples and sycamores.

"So what are your plans for the summer?"

"I haven't decided."

Vivian cast a curious glance as Andrea seemed more distracted than usual. Nevertheless, Vivian's upbeat tone didn't change.

"I was thinking that if you would like to spend the summer at home, perhaps an internship with the Sun Journal would be interesting. I could talk to Mr. Hall for you."

Andrea didn't answer.

~

Andrea was awarded an internship with the *Irish Examiner*, a newspaper in Cork, Ireland.

"When were you going to tell me about this?" Vivian asked.

"I wasn't sure I was going to get it."

The only photo taken of them since Andrea's childhood was on that day, arms at their sides and mouth-only smiles.

Chapter 36

Reflections

Vivian dramatically increased her smoking as did her worry that her secret could be exposed. Cork was only ten miles south of Monkstown.

Andrea had been in Ireland for six months when she received a letter.

> *Dear Andrea, I'm sorry to drop this on you so abruptly, but I can't seem to find any delicate way to communicate my condition to you. I've been diagnosed with lung cancer. It is neither treatable nor surprising.*
>
> *Some things need to be addressed as my time approaches. You will find additional funds in your account for your travel. I'm at home with a full-time hospice nurse. I ask that you make your arrangements as soon as you are able to do so. As*

the pain medications are increased, they, in return, diminish my ability to think clearly. Please let me know when you'll be arriving.

Love, Mother

~

Andrea got out of the taxi, tugged at her short skirt and tucked her hair behind one ear. She turned toward the house and saw her mother raise a hand from a first floor window.

Vivian could not make out the color of Andrea's travel bag; brown, sage, maybe taupe. It's certainly not the designer Red Fleur de Lis suitcase I gave her for the trip overseas, she thought.

At the top of the steps, several rows of newspapers were stacked along the gray-washed wood plank porch. Inside the back door, vases of various shapes and sizes congregated on the kitchen table. Several dispirited groups of once colorful flowers were now limp and sadly leaned over as if attempting to escape the murky, rank water which overpowered their once lovely fragrances.

A middle-aged woman, Andrea thought about fifty-five, appeared at the kitchen's entryway. The woman pinched her nose and grimaced. "I obviously haven't finished sprucing up in here."

Andrea felt her smile appeared genuine.

"You must be Andrea. I'm Barbara." She tilted her head to the side looking past Andrea. "Can I help you with your luggage?"

"I just brought one bag; thanks anyway."

"Your mother's bedroom is now in the study. I'm going to hang back while you two have some alone time."

Andrea continued ahead. The smells of medicines drifted throughout the house. The tick-tock of the grand hallway clock merged with the whispering of a distant respirator.

The compilation of these odors and sounds could lead to only the conclusion that death had made its camp here. Her heart started to beat faster.

Andrea walked into the living room and noticed that the clock had been moved. She followed the low pitch tone that led her closer to the study. Andrea glanced at her watch, then at the clock which seemed considerably smaller than when she was a child. She noted that the clock had not joined the recent time change. Andrea opened the glass door, stilled the pendulum and changed the hands to the correct time. One by one she pulled each of the three chains down while lifting its brass weights before tapping the pendulum. During her adolescent years this was one of the chores on her *to do* list.

The room her mother occupied was steps away.

Vivian's eyes were sallow, her pale skin had taken on a blue-grayish hue, and her wrists looked like brittle saplings. The breathing machine continually hissed a rhythm compatible with a light blue vein pulsating at her temple. Vivian opened her eyes and patted the bed. Andrea let out a shaky sigh and sat at the end.

Andrea's words seemed to run helter-skelter. "I'm sorry this is happening to you. Please tell me what I can do."

"I don't feel as bad as I look." Vivian uttered a huff. "You were dead right about those Viceroys."

Barbara walked in with a pitcher of water, refreshed Vivian's glass and held the straw to her mouth. She took a sip, barely able to swallow, cringed and waved her away. Barbara leaned Vivian forward and adjusted the oxygen tube as Andrea stood by.

Thank God Barbara is here, she thought.

Barbara picked up a sterling silver hairbrush from the bedside table and handed it to Andrea. She gave her a nod and left. Andrea moved closer and lightly brushed her mother's fine, sparse hair with delicate strokes.

"I used to brush your hair with this when you were a child," Vivian murmured. "You were captivated with the cameo and referred to her as the fancy white lady." Vivian rolled her eyes upward. "Do you remember, dear?"

"Yes, I remember. I'd sit at that old vanity and watch you in the mirror."

"And what were you thinking, dear?"

"I was thinking how ancient the brush looked with all its bristles bent over and also how gentle you were. You've always been gentle with me, and sometimes I wonder why I've always been a pain and never showed any appreciation for all you've done for me." Tears began to well up in Andrea's eyes, but she suppressed them.

Breathing her own inner turmoil, Vivian peered out the window and sighed. "The cancer is advanced, and the doctors have given me less than a month."

Andrea rolled her lips inward. "I'm sorry, Mother."

"I'm leaving you my estate. My attorney will be here later this afternoon to go over the necessary papers. Why don't you get settled in while I rest and we'll talk later."

Andrea leaned over, kissed Vivian on her forehead, and left the room.

This is the first time she has kissed me in years, Vivian thought. With a restful smile, she closed her eyes.

~

Andrea emerged from her mother's room and stood in the hallway where a blank canvas loomed before her. She heard Barbara rummaging in the kitchen.

Barbara pulled out a chair "I'm steeping some Earl Grey. Will you join me?"

Andrea picked up a cup and saucer with colorful floral bouquets and butterflies. She remembered the delicate pattern from so many years ago when her mother served "high tea" at the little table in Andrea's bedroom.

Barbara set a plate of muffins on the table and poured the tea. "I'm glad you're home to be a part of this process. People forget that death is a big part of life."

They sat in silence sipping tea and nibbling the sweets. It was Barbara's perception that brought Andrea around to the vast realization that she would need this woman during the weeks ahead.

Chapter 37

The Storm Finds Peace

Andrea stood at her mother's window, drew back the curtains and watched a couple of horses grazing in a nearby pasture.

"Andrea, I need to tell you something."

"What is it, Mother?"

"Please open the middle drawer to my vanity."

Vivian rotated her wrist and motioned with her forefinger. "Unwrap the key and open the trunk at the end of my bed."

Andrea discovered a pale blue linen handkerchief folded in half and in half again. Inside was an ornate key with knot work design. She inserted the key into the lock and turned it.

"Go ahead and lift the latch."

Andrea raised the lid. Her deep furrowed brow barely outweighed her narrowing eyes. "What's all this?"

Vivian swallowed with difficulty and continued. "Your grandparents brought the trunk and contents with them from

Ireland with the exception of a photo album. Your grandmother compiled the album for a wedding gift several years later."

Andrea sensed her mother's anguish, and Vivian squarely met her eyes. "Lift the blankets, and any questions you have will be answered."

Andrea removed the album, sat in a chair across the room and opened it. She turned pages featuring the magnificent estate and her grandmother's beautiful rose garden encompassed with dense lily of the valley. There was a sparkle in her eyes.

"Besides just the few photos I've seen of you, father and my grandparents, why haven't I seen this album until now?"

"I couldn't find a time to tell you the truth." Vivian looked away.

Andrea's shoulders stiffened and pulled back.

"What truth, Mother?"

Andrea hesitated at an oval-shaped photo. Her eyes fell upon a young bride and groom standing beneath an arbor encased with white and cream roses. They were attended by two witnesses; Vivian stood next to the bride.

"Who is that with my father?"

Vivian's troubled heart raced and her breath came quickly. "These photos are your true heritage, the history I denied you and is your birthright."

"I said who is that woman with my father?"

"That's Anna — your mother."

Andrea closed the album and stared over at Vivian. "You're not my mother?"

Vivian spoke in scant whispers. "I know I've wronged you, but my decision to act as your mother all these years was in your best interest. You must understand. I was handed a child who had no family. They were all gone. You had no one, and neither did I."

Andrea clutched the album tighter.

"I was in love with your father. He chose Anna, your mother, over me. After your family passed due to a fire, your grandfather asked me to raise you. I thought that one day I'd tell you everything. Instead, I grew into the role of your father's widow. It seemed to complete me, but there was a price — the lie to you."

Vivian's gaunt face contorted into a mixture of anguish and fear. "I have always loved you, Andrea. I often thought of the distance you maintained from me was surely my penalty. Had you really known the truth, I wonder if we would have been closer, but I was not willing to take the chance of losing you completely."

Andrea stood and embraced her new identity.

Vivian's voice quavered. "I'm asking you now to forgive me."

She bent over and hacked a persistent rough, croupy cough. Barbara came into the room, propped Vivian up against her pillows and gave her a sip of water.

"Please, just rest for now, Vivian." Barbara handed her a handkerchief and eyeballed Andrea on her way out.

Andrea tucked the album under her arm. "Forgive you? I just learned that my whole life has been a facade, so if you will forgive me, I don't know how I feel. You've given me a lot to digest, don't you think?"

Andrea walked to the end of the bed and stopped. "Incidentally, I have never loved anyone in my life, so don't feel left out."

She continued to the doorway and looked back. Her brows lifted, and she spoke with a barely audible tone.

"Now I understand why I don't look anything like you."

Andrea left the room, shut the door and braced herself along the other side.

Vivian lay her head back into the pillow and closed her eyes.

$\sim$

The next morning, Andrea woke to the sound of a whistling teakettle. She discovered Barbara at the kitchen table cradling a white porcelain cup of English breakfast and sipping the hot liquid.

"I've some raisin toast about to pop up. Would you care to join me?"

"No thanks. I'm going for a walk, maybe later."

Andrea slipped into her clogs. Although she had kicked them off the day before and completely missed the mud mat, they were now perfectly aligned along the wall with an array of boots and shoes. Surely Vivian's instructions, she thought.

Barbara soon stood beside her at the end of the stable corridor. Andrea leaned against the fence, her arms folded on top.

"All those years I assumed it was my fault for withholding any affection for her and always pushing her away. I often felt guilty though I did it not knowing why." Andrea bit her lip. "Now that she's dying, why did she feel the need to tell me at all?"

"When should she have told you? When you were a child? I have to say that under the circumstances, you might look at what your life would have been like without her. Think about it. What did Vivian do wrong? She gave you her love, a home to grow up in and advantages that most children aren't privileged to have. She truly loves you, Andrea." Barbara paused. "Well, I best get back and look in on her."

~

Andrea watched Barbara remove the oxygen tube and turn over the top edge of the bed sheet. She stroked Vivian's cheek and kissed her on the forehead.

Barbara laid her hand on Andrea's shoulder. "She didn't want it any longer. Her time is very near, but she can hear you. I'll be in the kitchen."

Andrea sat next to her mother and took her hand. Her eyes welled up. "I want you to know that I understand, and I'm thankful for the love you've shown me all these years. I also want to apologize for the way I treated you. I hope you'll forgive me. You were always there for me, and I'm here for you now. I love you, Mother."

The immense burden Vivian had harbored for over two decades gently lifted. A tranquil smile crossed her lips.

~

Vivian walked toward a cornfield and turned her face to the warming sun. Her body felt light. Her eyes began to glimmer. Towering cornstalks were being thrust from side to side. Her heart pounded with every sweep. The maze parted, he stepped out and flashed her that wide Irish grin that lasted and lasted.

Vivian was at peace.

Chapter 38

Walk In My Garden

Andrea stopped at an entrance bordered with imposing evergreens. Above, an arched sign read, Avonvale Horse Rescue.

Her car crept along the winding drive that led to a landscaped canvas of weeping willow trees, their branches swept to the ground. She stopped before the stables and stepped from her car.

He raised a ladle to his lips and took a slow drink.

"Well, if it isn't the bona fide veterinarian," she said. "And just what are *you* doing here?"

He tilted his head to one side with a pleasing smile. "I could ask you the same thing."

A pungent hickory scent drifted across the paddock. An old man hunched over a railing along the fence line.

"Hey, Sam, come on over here. I want you to meet someone."

Matthew turned to her. "The old guy knows his way around horses. He came with the place, a caretaker of sorts. In exchange for a roof over his head, I've kept him on to do stable chores."

Sam plodded over and turned to Andrea with a gleam in his eyes.

"Sam, this is Andrea. Her grandfather was Tom Clements."

The old man winked. "Welcome home, Lassie."

His voice crackled when he drew in a breath. Sam pulled down the brim of his cap and shuffled up The Green Road.

~

Once inside the bunkhouse, Sam pulled out a bottle from beneath his mattress. He took a long swig and scrubbed the back of his hand across his mouth. He stood upright, punched the air throwing back his head and let off a great laugh.

~

Andrea waved the air in front of her. "He smells awful. He has obviously been drinking."

"He's harmless and off duty," Matthew said.

"Are you aware that Mother passed?" she asked.

"Yes, I am. I'm sorry. Vivian was my shadow for a while after you left for Ireland. She talked incessantly about her time at Avonvale. Your family's history is remarkable; it's quite a story. What a tragedy at the end."

"I have a trunk full of family memorabilia that goes way back," Andrea said. "That's how I learned of the true story about Avonvale and my family."

"By the way, you left for Ireland rather abruptly. I was disappointed to learn of that after the fact. I thought you weren't to leave for weeks," Matthew said.

"My plans changed, and I didn't get the word around. Goodbyes aren't my forte." Andrea looked down and sighed. "I was insensitive in many areas of my life for a long time."

"You don't have to explain," he said.

"I imagine Vivian told you she wasn't my real mother, that she adopted me and swept us off to Boston after my grandfather died. Does any of this ring a bell?"

"She did, and she also shared the real estate section from a Rochester newspaper that indicated Avonvale was going up for auction. The article included a photograph of the property. I came to see it and fell in love with this place. When I returned to Boston, I told her I wanted to start up a horse rescue."

"I'm sure she was more than pleased about your news," Andrea said.

"She was, and then she said something I'll never forget. 'I know your head, your heart and your hands will always be with Avonvale.' Vivian was right, and along with her generous contribution, I bought the place and built these stables as she described them before the fire."

"Mother was very fond of you. Now I can see why," Andrea said.

"Without her faith in this undertaking, our horse rescue would not have been possible," he said.

"Our?"

"I couldn't have built this without her. Vivian will always be a part of Avonvale."

He shifted from one foot to the other. "We'll have lots of time to catch up. I've got some iced tea inside."

"Thank you. I'd like that," she said.

"Have you made any arrangements for a place to stay tonight?"

"No, I haven't. I came straight here."

"Andrea, you're welcome to stay at Avonvale. No worries. There's obviously plenty of room," he said with a warm smile.

"An iced tea sounds good," she said.

Once inside, Andrea paused at the kitchen window. "Mother had photos of my grandmother's rose garden. It was so beautiful at one time."

"It could be again, I suppose. I'm going to ride over to the south field and check on my mare who's about to foal. Would you like to go along?"

"I'll see you when you get back," she said.

"Feel free to look around. I won't be long."

Andrea stood in the rose garden. Her grandmother's rose bushes had been replaced with a twiggy undergrowth of briars and brambles from years of neglect. Lily of the valley had taken over the area and surrounded the gazebo.

Chapter 39

Reckoning

Andrea heard shouts coming from the stables and ran toward the horrific noise. She stopped at the entrance and peered around the corner.

Sam held a bottle up as if he were about to toast a celebration. "I'm not finished with you! I got me job back and your bungalow or didn't you notice. And now, your granddaughter to finish the job. What do you think of that?"

Andrea's heart picked up a faster rhythm.

Sam cocked his head to one side with a sneer. "And let's get one thing straight. It was the feckin' drink that went after Mary, not me." His voice was cracked and raw. "Tell her it wasn't supposed to be like that, won't you now."

He drank the pint dry, vehemently shook his head and cried out, "Well, I sure showed you, didn't I! I wasn't going to be thrown away as easy as that, you bleedin' maggot!" Sam smashed the bottle against the wall.

Just as quickly, he seemed to find a comfort in his confession. Sam hung his head, and his thoughts took him back to a place long ago, the only time when he felt someone's tenderness. Her grimy sunbaked skin accompanied her filmy eyes. She offered him a bun.

She said her name was Evelyn. "Get up and take a wee walk with me." She curled her arm in his. A rank smell emanated from her and blended with his own. He couldn't remember the last time someone had touched him. Even his mum rarely had any physical contact with him.

Sam remembered being sent off to wallow in the streets of Londonderry at age fourteen, and his father's last words echoed in Sam's throbbing head. "You're a no good git, and you'll never amount to anything. The drink is the only thing that will get us through life."

Even though Sam fought that very idea, he surrendered to his father's words over the years. It was easier than fighting for his life, and so, he would never really know what could have been. Solace was found in the bottle. Sam crawled in and stayed there; bottle, after bottle, after bottle. He could always blame the drink. Alcohol owned him.

Sam stumbled over to a stall, opened the door and dropped to his knees. He uncovered a pint of whiskey nestled in the straw, tipped his head back and downed several swallows. Andrea remained out of sight until he stood, grabbed a pitchfork and jabbed it at a horse in the stall. Scout tossed his head and pushed the air in his lungs through his nostrils.

Andrea stepped into the aisle. "Don't do this, Sam. We'll help you."

Sam stopped and waited for his glassy, bloodshot eyes to focus. "Aye, Lassie, maybe I won't for now and just maybe I will.

You see, I got to get even. I've nothing else left. Ask your almighty grandfather here."

She looked around. "Who?"

"What, are you blind? He's standing right there. He knew I set the fire but he couldn't prove it. I thought I took everything from that feckin' Irishman who had it all. His life should've been mine!"

Sam glared at her with a devious smile. "I had no choice, Lassie."

"What do you mean?" she asked.

Sam stifled a laugh and grabbed the stall door for support. "Your gran' didn't take to the likes of me. He wanted to kill me, and he could have with his bare hands. He left me with me face in the dirt, and I swore I'd get even. And you know what, Lassie? I did."

With downcast eyes, Sam took a long, loud breath. "But I just wanted to destroy the stables."

His mouth screwed into a knot and his chin tightened. "Those idiot horses kept running back in, and there was nothing I could do."

Sam's hostile expression slowly faded into a sheepish grin. "I'm an old man now, and I need your help." He reached his hand out. "Will you help me, Lassie?"

The look in his eyes said something else. Andrea backed away.

Harsh and angry breathing replaced any note of sincerity. "I was there when Dreamaker bolted back in. And, let me tell you, Andrew Wiley and his so-called champion horse were swallowed up in the flames!"

Sam guffawed and shook his fist in the air with a triumphant cry. "And Tom Clements never walked again! I might just as well poured gasoline into hell!"

He swigged down the rest and smashed the bottle against the stall door. Holding the jagged neck in front of him, he turned and faced Andrea. Scout whinnied and reared up. The first flying hoof thrust Sam to the floor. The second strike hit him squarely on the back of his skull.

It was over.

Andreas's attention was diverted to the end of the stable isle.

A brown felt fedora with a black grosgrain ribbon band hung on the swinging gable door.

A skylark trilled.